TIME IS MONEY
(An Anthony Stone Novel)

A novel

SILK WHITE

Good2Go Publishing

Published by:
GOOD2GO PUBLISHING
7311 W. Glass Lane
Laveen, AZ 85339
www.good2gopublishing.com
Twitter @good2gobooks
G2G@good2gopublishing.com
Facebook.com/good2gopublishing
ThirdLane Marketing: Brian James
Brian@good2gopublishing.com

Cover design: Davida Baldwin
Editor: Kesha Buckhana
ISBN: 978-0692275962

BOOKS BY THIS AUTHOR

Married To Da Streets

Never Be the Same

Stranded

Tears of a Hustler

Tears of a Hustler 2

Tears of a Hustler 3

Tears of a Hustler 4

Tears of a Hustler 5

Tears of a Hustler 6

Teflon Queen

Teflon Queen 2

Teflon Queen 3

Teflon Queen 4

Time Is Money *(An Anthony Stone Novel)*

48 Hours to Die *(An Anthony Stone Novel)*

ACKNOWLEDGMENTS

To all of you who are reading this, thank you for stepping inside the bookstore, stopping by the library, or downloading a copy of Time Is Money. I hope you have enjoyed this read from top to bottom. My goal is to get better and better with each story. I want to thank everyone for all their love and support. It is definitely appreciated!

Now without further ado Ladies and Gentleman, I give you **"Time Is Money."** ENJOY!

$iLK WHiTE

PROLOGUE

G host slammed the clip into the base of the M-16 rifle in which he held and then rolled his Bill Clinton mask down over his face. He looked around the back of the van at his two partners in crime who all wore black, and a bulletproof vest resting over the top of their shirts.

"Dana, no unnecessary gunfire this time please," Ghost said, giving his little sister a hard stare.

"Last time wasn't my fault," Dana said, as she pulled her Obama mask down over her face. At the last heist, a guard caught himself trying to be a hero and save the day. Thanks to Dana, he was quickly rewarded with a bullet right between the eyes.

Ghost looked over at the man who sat next to Dana. "Dougie you ready to roll?"

"I'm as ready as can be," he said flashing a nervous smile, as he pulled down his Ronald Reagan mask, grabbing the two large duffle bags that rested down at his feet. Dougie's job was to snatch as much money as he could while Ghost and Dana took care of the rest. They gave him the name 'Dougie' because he was good at and loved doing the Dougie dance, so the name kind of stuck with him.

Ghost called out to the driver, "Hey Randy you keep this motherfucker running!" The last thing Ghost needed was to come running out the bank and have to lose valuable seconds waiting for the car to start.

Randy gave him a head nod as he watched the trio hop out the back of the van and enter the bank.

TIME IS MONEY

(An Anthony Stone Novel)

1
TIME IS MONEY

"**H**ow you doing today Ms. Evans," the bank guard politely asked the elderly woman. He'd been working at this bank for the last three years and he loved his job.

"I'm doing well. How about yourself?"

"Just hanging in there," the guard said with a smile.

"I'm just happy to see another day." He was getting ready to say something else, but the words got caught in his throat when he saw a man wearing a Bill Clinton mask carrying an assault rifle, followed by another gunman wearing an Obama mask enter the bank.

"Get the fuck on the floor now!" Bill Clinton yelled, scaring everyone in the bank. He roughly slammed the guard down on the floor and removed the man's pistol from his holster.

Obama held two silenced 9mms and aimed them at two of the clerks that stood behind the counter. Once everything was under control, Ronald Reagan hopped over the counter, grabbed one of the clerk's by her blonde hair, and smacked the shit out of her. "Bitch, take me to the safe right now!" Scared to death, the clerk did as she was told.

"Everybody stay calm and nobody gets hurt!" Bill Clinton yelled, keeping everybody in line. He quickly glanced down at his watch. Forty seconds had passed since the time they stepped foot in the bank.

Once in the safe area, Ronald Reagan shoved the blonde haired clerk down to the floor, as he began to fill up the two duffle bags quickly. He held the bag open with one hand, while he shoveled money into the bag with his other hand. Once the first bag was filled, he quickly grabbed the second bag, but stopped abruptly when he heard in his earpiece that a silent alarm had been pulled on his police scanner. "Oh shit!" he said, as he ran back out to the front of the bank. "We got trouble! Somebody pulled the silent alarm!"

"We still got three minutes before the cops show up! We'll be gone in two! Go grab as much money as you can in one minute!" Bill Clinton told him. "Let's go! Time is money!" he yelled, looking down at his watch.

Obama looked at the other clerk and noticed the nervous look on her face. "You pulled that alarm?"

"I'm sorry," the clerk said, as tears ran down her face. "Please don't hurt me. I have a fam..." Obama put a bullet in her head before she could even finish her sentence. Obama then turned his gun on the next clerk and put a bullet between her eyes as well. Before that clerk's body even got a chance to hit the floor, he was already on to the next clerk.

"Time!" Bill Clinton yelled. Instantly Ronald Reagan emerged from the back with a duffle bag strapped over both shoulders. Bill Clinton then yelled, "Triangle Offense!"

Obama quickly headed towards the door making sure the coast was clear in the front, while Bill Clinton brought up the rear and power walked backwards making sure the coast was clear from behind while protecting the money man that rested in between the two.

Once outside, the trio hopped in the van and Randy quickly put the pedal to the metal and left tire marks in front of the bank. Randy drove fifteen blocks away and pulled into an underground parking garage, where all four of them hopped out the van and into separate cars.

Ghost snatched the Bill Clinton mask from his face and grabbed one of the duffle bags while Dougie removed his Ronald Reagan mask and grabbed the other bag. Dana removed the Obama mask from her face and leapt in an Acura that awaited her.

"Everyone meet at the safe house in an hour!" Ghost said, as he pulled out of the parking garage first followed by Randy, Dana, and then Dougie.

2
STICKY SITUATION

Detective Anthony Stone pulled up to the scene and could immediately tell by how much press was out in front of the bank, that whatever had happened, it wasn't good. It was a media circus out there. Reporters hovered along the outskirts of the police barrier, buzzing and speculating on what had happened. Stone pushed his way through the reporters and ducked under the yellow tape, heading towards the bank when he was stopped by a white uniform officer.

"Back behind the tape now!" an officer yelled. "This is a crime scene here!"

"Yeah I know dick head," Stone said as he flashed his badge and brushed pass the officer. Stone's white t-shirt and sagging jeans must have thrown off the officer.

"I'm so sorry about that detective," the officer quickly apologized.

Stone waved the officer silent and walked over to where he saw his captain standing with an angry face. "Hey Captain how's it looking?"

"Not good; not good at all!" the captain barked. "This is the fourth bank these fuckers have hit in the last two months!" he fumed.

"You sure it's the same crew?" Stone asked, looking around at the mayhem and destruction that was left behind.

"Positive!" the captain barked. "You're my best detective and I want you on this case."

"Captain Fisher, I have a lot on my plate right now. Are you sure you want me on this case?" Stone asked. The last time Captain Fisher had personally assigned

Detective Stone to a case things ended in a high speed chase with two hostages murdered.

"Stone you're my only hope right now," Captain Fisher said. "You may be a wild card, but right now you're our only shot at catching these fuckers."

Stone had heard about the series of bank robberies that had taken place over the last few months. Three violent gunmen walked into a bank, took all their money, and murdered at least two victims in less than two minutes, each time. The police had no clue who the gunmen were, but Stone planned on getting to the bottom of it. "I need to see the tapes."

Captain Fisher walked Anthony Stone in the back where the surveillance cameras were held. "These animals have to be stopped!" Captain Fisher fumed. Anthony Stone sat down in a fold out chair and watched the tapes carefully. The first thing he noticed was that the trio were unusually organized and they weren't afraid to kill if they had too. He also noticed that the trio never stayed inside a bank for longer than four minutes, making it even more difficult for authorities to catch them red handed. Whoever the gunmen were, they seemed to be very clever. "Hold on! Stop the tape!" Stone yelled out. "Rewind it back about ten seconds."

When the tape played over, Stone noticed that the gunman wearing the Obama mask had a nice ass and some thick thighs. "Obama is a woman," he called out.

"How can you be so sure?" Captain Fisher asked.
"Look at that ass," Stone said smiling. Everyone knew he was an action freak, but he was also a ladies man. "And check out those thighs."

"So our shooter is a woman," Captain Fisher said. "Look in our database and see if we can find a woman that meets those measurements that has a criminal record."

"You got it boss," a uniform cop said as he left to go handle the task.

"Mind if I borrow this tape?" Stone asked.

"I'll have a copy on your desk first thing in the morning," Fisher's voice boomed, as he exited the back room.

Stone walked around the bank and looked for anything that may help him crack the case. In the video, he noticed that one of the gunmen went straight to the woman who had the key to the safe, which meant that they had done their homework and knew exactly who to go after. Stone exited the bank saying goodbye to his captain and hopped in his all black Charger. Once inside his ride, Stone reached in his glove compartment and removed a bottle of Tequila. He quickly turned the bottle up to his lips. "Damn!" he growled with his face crumbled. Unlike other detectives, Anthony Stone worked better with a little drink in his system.

Stone cruised aimlessly through the city and on his lap, sat the bottle of Tequila. All that was on his mind was tracking down the bank robbers. He knew it wouldn't be easy, but this type of case had his name written all over it. Just from looking at the surveillance tape, he could tell that the bank robbers would never go down quietly or without deadly force.

Stone pulled up in front of his apartment building, as a domestic call came through his radio. Since the location wasn't far from his apartment, he decided to take the call. "I'm on it," he said into his walkie-talkie and headed towards the location. Outside of work, Anthony Stone didn't have much of a life. It was just one case after another.

Stone pulled up in front of the building, hopped out, and entered the building. Rather than wait for the elevator, Stone decided it would be best to take the stairs. He stepped out the staircase and walked down the narrow hallway until he reached the door.

KNOCK! KNOCK! KNOCK!

Seconds later, a tall black man cracked the door, peeking out. "Yeah was sup?"

"Yeah I got a call about a disturbance," Stone said as he noticed fresh scratches on the man's neck and shoulder.

"Nah ain't no disturbance over here!" The man went to close the door, but Stone quickly stuck his foot in the doorway before it could close.

"Sir, I'm going to have to come in and see your girlfriend!" Stone said sternly. The man reluctantly allowed Detective Stone inside the apartment.

Stone stepped foot in the apartment and the first thing he noticed was that the place was a mess. There were clothes thrown everywhere with trash lying around all over the floor.

"There she goes, you happy?" the man's voice boomed.

Stone looked at the chick sitting on the couch and noticed dots of blood on the floor near her along with a few bruises around her eye and neck area. "Ma'am, are you okay?"

The woman looked down at the floor and nodded her head yes. Stone then turned his gaze back over to the man. "Put a shirt on! You're coming with me!"

"For what?" the man asked, as if he didn't know what he had done wrong.

"I'm not going to tell you again!" Stone told him as he took a step forward. Without warning, the man made a dash for the front door. Stone quickly took off after the man, tackling him in the hallway right before he reached the door.

The man spun around and delivered an elbow that connected with Stone's chin. The blow stunned Stone and allowed the man a chance to make it back to his feet. He quickly tried to put Stone in a *UFC* style chokehold. The tall man quickly dropped down to the floor, wrapped his legs around Stone's waist, and applied more pressure to the chokehold. "That's right motherfucker go to sleep!" the man growled.

Stone did his best to escape the chokehold, but the more he fought, the weaker he became. Having no other choice, Stone reached in his pocket and removed a pocket knife. The blade popped out with a snap as he drove it back into the man's side. He did that repeatedly until the man released his grip on the chokehold. Stone quickly made it to his feet and unloaded a twelve punch combination into the man's face. Stone was about to stomp the man out, when out of nowhere, the man's girlfriend hopped on Stone's back and began clawing at Stone's face.

"Bitch!" Stone barked as he bent over and violently flung the girl over his shoulders down onto the glass coffee table that rested in the living room. He bent the woman's arm back and hand cuffed her. Stone looked up and saw the man coming towards him, holding the pocket knife. Stone quickly pulled his P89 from his holster and shot the man in his thigh. He watched as the man crumbled down to the floor clutching his leg.

"Hands behind your back!" Stone ordered, as he quickly cuffed the tall man and called for backup.

3

I NEED YOU FOCUSED

Dana sat at a red light as the sound of Trey Songz hummed softly through her speakers at a reasonable volume. Ghost had called a meeting as he always did when it was time to split up the money. Dana was in no hurry to get to the meeting because she was sure Ghost was going to tear into her ass about her opening fire on the clerks that pulled the silent alarm. Dana knew she shouldn't have shot the clerks, but in the heat of the moment, it seemed like the right thing to do. By them pushing that silent alarm they were trying to end Dana's life so she figured why not return the favor.

Dana was a regular girl who'd been through a lot over the years. A few situations that had occurred in her life turned her heartless, and after both of her parents died in a car crash; Dana no longer wanted to live. The only person that was there for her after her parents died was her brother, Ghost. Ghost was hard on her, but she knew it was only because he wanted the best for her.

Dana pulled into the driveway of the house that Ghost used for meetings. The only thing this house was only used for other than meetings was addressing anything that went wrong on a job. If something happened, this was the meet up spot. Other than that, the house was never used for any other reason.

Dana stepped foot in the house and the first person she saw sitting at the round table was Dougie. Dougie was always the type to be laughing, dancing, and joking around. When Dana saw the serious look on his face, she knew she was in big trouble. The next person she saw at the round table was Randy. In his hand, he held a cigarette and in front of him, sat a glass of dark liquor. As usual, he had a nonchalant look on his face. The truth was Randy envied Dana because he felt that since she was the only woman on the team, she should have been the driver instead of him, but that decision wasn't up to him, it was up to Ghost. Last but not least, Dana spotted Ghost sitting at the round table. He wore a custom made fitted grey suit with a slim tie to match. Sitting in front of him was a glass of dark liquor.

"Listen Ghost I know you're upset but...."

"Sit yo ass down!" Ghost's voice boomed cutting Dana off. He was so mad with her that if she wasn't his sister he might have put his hands on her.

"So far we have successfully robbed four banks," Ghost began. "Thanks to my perfect planning and Randy's great driving skills," he paused for a second. "When I came up with these plans, I don't think murder was a part of it," he said with his gaze falling on Dana. "We are not murderers and we only use our weapons if we have to, if we're forced to, or when we're left with no other choice." He paused to take a sip from his drink and to look at Dana. "Four bank robberies and you've killed six people."

"Ghost I know you're mad with me, but you have to give me a chance to explain," Dana said. "When we go up in these banks, everyone needs to know that we ain't fucking around," she said. "And when those clerks pushed the silent alarm, I felt as if they didn't respect us, so I did what I had to do so the next time we walk into a bank, the clerks will know that we are not fucking around and think twice about pushing the silent alarm."

"We're not taking down banks for a reputation! We're taking them down so we can get paid!" Ghost reminded her. "The more you use your gun during a job, the more the cops are going to be gunning for us, and instead of them trying to arrest us; they'll be trying to put us down."

"Fuck the police!" Dana spat. "Since when did we start giving a fuck about them?"

"I don't give a fuck about the police and you all know that. You guys are the only family I got and I'm not trying to lose y'all because we're known as the armed and dangerous bank robbers," he pointed out. "Now if the cops force our hand, then that's different. We'll air their asses out in a heartbeat, but until that time comes, do not use your gun during a job again unless you are left with no other choice." Ghost glared at his little sister. "Do I make myself clear?"

"Yes," Dana mumbled with a slight attitude. She hated how cautious Ghost was. He always wanted to plan and be prepared for things, but in there line of work sometimes things didn't always go according to plan.

Ghost stood up and neatly stacked the money in front of each member that sat at the table. He sat Randy's money down in front of him and said. "A big part of our success is you and your driving skills. I know sometimes you want to go inside the banks with us where all the action is, but you are the best driver I know and I need you behind that wheel."

Randy nodded his head. "It's all good Ghost. I'm pretty sure I'll get my chance to get a piece of the action one day."

"One day," Ghost smiled. "You all know the rules. Don't go out spending like crazy and making big purchases. We stay low key and under the radar."

Dougie looked down at his share of the money, hopped up and broke out into a dance. He was smiling from ear to ear as he did the latest dance moves that the young kids were now doing these days. Before Ghost had recruited Dougie, he was working at a fast food restaurant. When Ghost would walk into the restaurant he would always see the hunger in Dougie's eyes and one day he decided to give him a shot in the big leagues and Dougie had been rocking with Ghost ever since. Dougie's job was to collect the money while Ghost and Dana did all the dirty work. "I love you Ghost!" Dougie said as he hugged Ghost and tried to get him to dance, but of course, Ghost was too cool to dance. Ghost was strictly about business most of the time.

"What's next for us?" Dana asked. She was still in kind of a salty mood, but she continued to keep her face neutral.

Ghost smiled as he reached under the table and pulled out a blueprint. "Next we take down an armored truck."

"Are you serious?" Dougie asked. He was no longer laughing and joking. He was now dead serious.

"Yes, I'm as serious as cancer," Ghost continued. "We're going to catch them when they make their last pick up for the day downtown. I've been scoping out their routes for the past two weeks and everything is like clockwork," he smiled. "There are three men to a truck. The two guards in the back carry shotguns and the third man is the driver."

"Sounds like a suicide mission to me," Randy said, stumping his cigarette out and helping himself to another glass of liquor.

"We have a four minute window to make this happen," Ghost told them. "These guards are trained to shoot first and ask questions never, so this job may call for us to use force," he said looking over at Dana. "If we all stick to the plan, I can promise you all that no one will get hurt; well at least not any of us," he chuckled. "Who all in?"

Ghost watched his entire crew all raised their hands. "Great! This job will require us to use two cars. Half the money will go in one car and the other half in the other. We get away safely and we meet back up here. If anybody gets caught, keep your fucking mouth shut and we'll hold your money. I'll be riding with Randy on this job and Dana you'll be riding with Dougie. We taking this truck down in two days so be ready."

4
I NEED A DRINK

After the meeting was over, Dana hopped in her car, merged onto the highway, and just drove. Whenever she needed to escape life, get away for a second, and think, the highway was her answer. It was something about driving, listening to calm R&B music that relaxed Dana's mind and put her at ease. During her ride, Ghost's words replayed repeatedly in her head. He had a few good points but Dana still felt as if she had done the right thing by shooting the clerks at the bank. All over the radio and on every T.V. station they were talking about the armed and dangerous bank robbers. From what

Dana was hearing the cops had no clue as to who the bank robbers were. In the type of business Dana was in, that was a good thing. No news was always good news. After driving around for a little over an hour, Dana came across a nice low-key looking lounge. She wasn't really the partying type, but tonight she could really use a drink and she wouldn't mind listening to a little music either.

Dana exited her car and headed towards the entrance of the lounge where a bulldog-looking dike looked at Dana as if she couldn't wait to frisk her. Dana was 5'6" and weighed about 150 lbs. People said she favored the actress Lauren London.

"Spread your arms and turn around!" the female bouncer said with authority as she proceeded to frisk Dana. While frisking Dana, the female bouncer made sure when she reached Dana's curves that she gave them a little extra attention.

After being semi-molested, Dana was finally allowed to enter the lounge. She hadn't planned on going out so she wasn't properly dressed for the occasion. While all the other women in the club wore tight fitting skimpy attire, Dana strolled in wearing a pair of tight black jeans and a black wife-beater. On her feet, she wore a pair of flat, open-toe sandals, her hair was pulled back into a ponytail, and a pair of oversized designer shades hid her eyes. Not really in a party mood, Dana headed straight for the bar. She sat on the only available open stool and ordered a shot of Vodka. Dana downed the glass of liquid fire in one gulp and raised her hand to flag down the bartender so she could order another drink, when out of nowhere the man sitting next to her shoved his bottle of Pineapple Cîroc towards her.

"Help yourself," the man who sat next to her told her.

Dana looked the man up and down. She had to admit he was definitely easy on the eyes and the type of man that she would give the time of day, but of course, she had to put up a front. "Excuse you, but I can afford my own drink," she said in a snappy tone.

"I never said you couldn't," the man countered in a smooth tone and proceeded to fill Dana's glass up anyway. "They say it's not good to drink by yourself and from the looks of things," he said, giving Dana a once over, "you can use this drink just as much as me."

Dana looked at the handsome man and smiled. "First of all, I don't drink with strangers and second of all there's no telling where your mouth has been."

"Stone," the handsome man said extending his hand.

"Dana," she said shaking his hand with little effort.

"Now that we're no longer strangers," Stone paused to down his shot. "Drink up."

"Haven't been doing anything with your mouth that I need to know about; have you?" Dana teased as she downed the shot and then made an ugly face.

"There are plenty of things I can do with this mouth and if you be nice, I may even give you the Stone special," he said, openly flirting with her.

Dana smiled and refilled her glass. "You've got my attention. What's the Stone special?"

Stone returned her smile. "I said *if* you be nice."

"Well I'm about to be on my best behavior," she joked. It had been a long time since Dana had laughed like this. Due to her work, she usually was in a bitter and serious mood. In her line of business, there was no time to joke or laugh. It was all business all the time so tonight Dana decided that she would take a night out to enjoy herself.

Stone smiled. "You have some nice lips."

Dana licked them seductively. "You think so?"

"Thinking is for people that are not sure," Stone replied as he stood up, grabbed Dana's hand, and led her out to the dance floor. "This is my song."

"No," Dana weakly protested, but finally gave in. For a moment, Dana felt as if her and Stone were the only two in the lounge. Stone pulled her close to him and gripped her hips as the two made love on the dance floor with their clothes on. Dana wrapped her arms around Stone's neck and swayed her hips to the beat pumping through the speakers. During the dance, Stone put his lips on Dana's neck and began to kiss slowly. Dana closed her eyes and lightly moaned. She knew what was happening was wrong, but for some strange reason it felt so right. Stone's hands felt perfect on her body.

Out of nowhere, Dana grabbed Stone's face and kissed him. When she realized what she had done, she quickly apologized. "I'm sorry! I've never acted like this and I don't know what came over me!"

"Nothing to apologize for." Stone smiled as the two made their way back over to their stools. Stone placed his hand on Dana's thigh and gave it a slight massage. "I like you."

Dana sucked her teeth. "You don't even know me and don't think because I let you kiss me that you getting some pussy either."

Stone smiled. "I would love to get to know you; maybe take you out if that's okay with you."

"That may be able to be arranged," Dana said, playing hard to get, but the truth was she wanted Stone way more than she wanted to admit.

"I'll be right back. I need to go use the restroom," Stone said as he got up and headed towards the restroom. Not even twenty seconds after Stone left, a man with a baby afro and a Hulk Hogan mustache sat in his seat.

"I'm sorry, but my friend was sitting there and he'll be back in a second. He just went..."

"Listen baby you move ya feet and you lose ya seat," the man with the afro said in a quick pimp like tone. "You've talked to the rest now talk to the best."

"Are you serious?" Dana asked. She wanted to make sure this wasn't a joke before she hurt the man's feelings.

"As a heart attack baby," the man with the afro said. "I'm saying though; why don't we get out of here and make some history tonight?"

Before Dana had a chance to reply, Stone walked up right on time. "Excuse me fam," he said politely. "But I think you're sitting in my seat."

The man with the afro turned and looked at Stone as if he was crazy. "This is a free motherfucking country so I can sit where I damn well please!"

Without warning Stone turned and slapped fire out of the man's hand. Before he got a chance to recover, Stone kicked the stool from up under the man and watched him crash down to the sticky lounge floor.

"You come over here trying to disrespect my shorty?" Stone growled as he raised his foot and stomped the man's head down into the floor. He did that repeatedly until two beefy bouncers came over and roughly escorted him out of the club.

Dana looked down at the man with the afro, raised her foot, and stomped his head down into the floor one last time before heading outside to go catch up with Stone.

SILK WHITE

5
NIGHT CAP

Once outside of the lounge Stone was getting ready to start a fight with the two bouncers that tossed him out when Dana quickly persuaded him to let it go. "Don't let them ruin our night," she said, intertwining her arm with his. They walked down the block until they reached Dana's cocaine white Benz.

Stone looked at Dana as if she had lost her mind. "I'm not letting you drive in this condition. I'll call you a cab."

"And what about you?" Dana asked. "If I can't drive, then you can't either. You've had more to drink than me."

Stone smiled. "I think there's a motel around here somewhere that I can crash at for the night."

"Boy please," Dana said shaking her head. "I'm not letting you stay at no motel. We can both just take a cab to my place and crash there for the night," she suggested.

"You sure that will be alright?" Stone asked. "Because I don't have time to be fighting off no old crazy boyfriends; not tonight."

"Thankfully for you, I don't have a boyfriend or no crazy ex-boyfriends. It's just me, myself, and I," Dana said smiling as she flagged down a cab. Stone and Dana piled into the back of a cab and made small talk for the entire ride until the cab pulled up in front of a baby mansion.

Stone stepped out of the cab and looked up at her home. "Damn this is a nice place," he pointed out.

"Why thank you," Dana said as she intertwined her arm with his and led him to the front door. Instead of using a key, Dana typed in a code on the keypad and the door opened. "Okay make yourself at home," Dana said as she kicked off her shoes and walked through the house barefoot.

Stone walked through the house admiring its beauty and all of the expensive things inside. He would have to work one hundred years to ever be able to afford a place as nice Dana's. "This is a nice place you have here," he complimented.

"Yeah my parents left me and my brother a nice piece of change when they died," she lied.

"Sorry to hear that."

"It's okay. You want a sandwich or anything?" Dana asked, quickly changing the subject.

"Nah I'm good. Just show me to the couch and I'll be good," Stone said. He had to get up early and begin working on the bank robber's case. Stone was eager to sink his teeth into the case and take them down.

Dana laughed. "I do have a guest bedroom you know."

"Yeah I know. I just didn't want you to have to go through no extra trouble or..." Stone was cut off when Dana invaded his personal space and kissed him once more.

Stone and Dana's tongues did a slow dance as Stone's hands explored Dana's ass. While the two kissed, Dana helped remove Stone's shirt. Dana's eyes lit up when she saw how chiseled and cut up Stone's body was. He had the body of an athlete. Stone scooped Dana up in the air and she quickly wrapped her legs around Stone's waist as he carried her over to the couch. Stone roughly tossed Dana down onto the couch and removed her clothes. When Stone saw Dana's freshly waxed fat pussy looking up at him, he could no longer control himself. Stone got down on his knees, opened Dana's legs as wide as they could go, and dove in face first. He started with slow wet kisses that turned into licks. Stone licked Dana's pussy, like a cat drinking milk, as if her juices would somehow better his life.

"Oh my God!" Dana moaned good and long. She moaned as she moved up and down, her movements slow and intense. She grinded her hips as her legs automatically locked around Stone's head. After Stone felt Dana's leg shiver, he slid in between her legs missionary style, face to face and tongue to tongue. The two kissed like sloppy animals as Stone eased himself inside of Dana. From how tight Dana's box was; Stone could tell that she hadn't been sexually active in a while. "Harder!" Dana demanded in a low growl. Stone sucked on Dana's bottom lip as he pumped in and out of her walls. Dana's moans told him that she wanted more and Stone gave her just that.

Stone moved Dana from the couch down to the floor, forcing her to lie on her stomach as he entered her from behind. He fucked her as hard as he could. He could feel sweat gathering on his neck and back and he continued to fuck her the way she kept telling him to, harder. "Like that?" Stone spat as he slapped Dana's ass with force.

Dana moaned and then whispered. "I'm about to come again."

When Stone heard that, he sped up his strokes until he couldn't take it anymore and erupted spilling his fluids on Dana's ass.

From there Stone laid flat on his back while Dana curled up and rested her head on his chest. The two laid like that in complete silence until they both drifted off to sleep.

6

DECISIONS

Ghost walked through the LAX airport dressed in a tailor fitted, grey *Armani* suit and a slim black tie. He stood 6 feet and 1 inch tall and favored the actor Mekhi Phifer. Ghost was always dressed to impress, but as usual, his mind was on business. He took a flight all the way to Los Angeles to talk business with some big time investor that went by the name, Brent Harrington. Brent was supposed to be the man to see if you had a lot of illegal money and you were looking to invest and clean it up.

Ghost exited the airport and slid in the back seat of the limousine that awaited his arrival. During the ride, he helped himself to a drink and blankly stared out the window. Ghost had a lot on his mind and if everything with the *Brinks* truck job went smoothly, he'd finally be able to retire. That was his sole purpose of having the meeting with Brent; he was setting up all the right moves so that once it was all over he'd be able to ride off into the sunset without a financial care in the world.

The limousine pulled up in front of a huge mansion. The driver quickly walked around to the back door and opened it. Ghost stepped foot out the back of the limousine and was immediately greeted by Brent Harrington.

"Brent it's a pleasure to meet you," Ghost extended his hand.

"The pleasures all mines," Brent said giving Ghost's hand a firm shake. "How was your flight?"

"Can't complain."

"Come with me," Brent said as the two entered the mansion.

"I hope my driver met your every last need."

Ghost smiled. "Yes he sure did."

"Great," Brent said as he led Ghost down the elementary school sized hallway. The mansion looked big enough to fit twenty families inside. He led Ghost to a sitting area that held a fireplace.

"Your house is beautiful," Ghost complimented as he and Brent both sat. Seconds later, a maid walked into the room, carrying two drinks on a silver platter. Brent and Ghost took the drinks and then got straight down to business.

"Let me get straight to the point," Ghost began. "I have a lot of money that I'm looking to invest, but I want to make sure you're the right person to do this with," he sipped his drink slowly.

"I can assure you Mr. Ghost that I'm your man," Brent smiled. "My team and I have several businesses where your money can sit and gain interest."

"Several businesses like?" Ghost asked. He was looking to invest a few million so he had to be sure that everything that Brent said was legit.

"Mc Donald's, Chase Bank, stocks, clubs, NFL, and NBA teams... I could go on and on. You name it and my team and I can make it happen," Brent smiled and then downed his drink in one gulp and almost instantly his maid showed up with two more drinks on a silver platter.

Ghost finished his drink and then grabbed the next one. "What I need to know is, is there any way this can go wrong? Because I'm going to trust you with all my money and I had to work extremely hard to get this money, so I just want to be sure that everything will work out like you say it will." Ghost sipped his drink.

Brent chuckled. "Ghost I can assure you, you have nothing to worry about. Every month you will receive an update of what's going on and if one business starts to act funny or ask too many questions, then we just move that portion of money to another business and keep it moving. There's no way to lose."

Ghost sipped his drink. "What's in it for you?"

"Twenty percent," Brent smiled greedily.

"Fifteen," Ghost countered quickly.

"The price is nonnegotiable," Brent told him. "How much are you looking to invest?"

"Two million."

"Okay so two hundred thousand won't hurt you," Brent smiled. "Why don't you go back home and think about it for a few days and then get back to me."

"Nothing to think about. I'm going to invest with you." Ghost's face suddenly became serious. "Brent this is all the money that I have to my name and I'm trusting you to do what you say you are going to do."

Brent chuckled. "Ghost you're only looking to invest two million dollars; no disrespect, but I piss two million dollars. Trust me you're in good hands," he extended his hand.

Ghost looked at Brent for a few seconds before he finally shook his hand finalizing the deal.

7
SHOW TIME

Dana sat in the passenger seat of a stolen black *Charger*, with a tech-9 resting on her lap and behind the wheel sat Dougie. They were parked two blocks away from where the armored truck was supposed to make its last pick up for the day.

Dougie looked down at his watch. "Ten minutes til show time."

Dana didn't respond. Her mind was stuck on the wonderful time that her and Stone had the other night. She couldn't remember the last time she had such a good time.

They laughed, joked, danced, and drank the night away as if they had known one another for years. Dana's only problem was that she feared that she may have gave up the goodies too fast and that maybe she would never hear from Stone again. *"What if he never calls because he thinks I'm a hoe?"* she asked herself. Negative thoughts floated around in her mind and right now, she needed to be focused.

"You heard me?" Dougie asked, snapping Dana out of her thoughts. "I said two minutes til show time." His glance lingered on Dana for a few seconds longer. "You alright?"

"Yeah I'm good. Let's do this," Dana said rolling the President Obama mask down over her face and then making sure her weapon was ready for action.

*****

Four blocks away, Randy sat behind the wheel of a black *Camaro* with a no nonsense look on his face. He knew how important this day was, not to mention it was a good chance that his driving skills were going to be put to the ultimate test today. Over in the passenger seat sat Ghost. He too had the look of no nonsense look on his face as an M-16 rested on his lap. The only thing on his mind was completing the mission at hand, especially since he had already transferred Brent the two million dollars. Being completely broke; Ghost now had to do what he had to do. This last mission would set Ghost straight financially, allowing him to be able to live off of the money from the heist, while Brent flipped his retirement money for him.

"Here we go," Ghost said, as he watched the armored truck pull up to the side of the bank. He quickly pulled the Bill Clinton mask down over his face and held his weapon in a firm grip. His entire future depended on this one job. Ghost watched as the truck pulled up to the side of the bank. Two armed guards hopped out and entered the bank. "Let's go!"

Randy quickly stomped down on the gas pedal and the *Camaro* leaped into action. Once the *Camaro* was in a close enough range, Randy stomped down on the brakes and cut the wheel hard to the right. The *Camaro* sat in front of the armored truck at a weird angle. Seconds later a black *Charger* did the same exact thing from behind boxing the armored truck in.

Ghost quickly hopped out of the Camaro and aimed his M-16 at the driver. He immediately saw that the driver got on his radio and called for backup. In a regular situation, Ghost would have shot the driver instantly, but today he knew the driver hid behind bulletproof glass.

Behind the truck, Dana jumped out the passenger seat of the Charger and headed straight for the back door of the truck. She snatched it open with one hand, stuck her tech-9 inside the back of the truck with her other hand, and squeezed the trigger, killing the backup guard that rested in the back of the truck. Once the guard was down, Dana hopped up on the back of the truck and began grabbing bags of money. She hopped down off the back of the truck just as the two armed guards were making their way back out of the bank.

Before the two guards got a chance to do anything, Ghost quickly gunned them both down. He then ran over and quickly grabbed the bags of money that the guards were carrying. He looked up and saw Dana jump in the back seat of the *Charger* with the money. Instantly, the *Charger* was headed in the opposite direction at a breaking speed.

Ghost ran back to the *Camaro* and hopped in the front seat. "We out!"

Randy stomped down on the gas pedal, and the *Camaro* roared and took flight. There was a big parking garage about seven blocks ahead. In the garage, the real getaway car awaited their arrival. All they had to do was get there unseen.

SILK WHITE

8
CHANGE OF PLANS

Stone sat, double parked in front of a liquor store. Positioned in between his legs was a half empty bottle of orange juice. He quickly added some Vodka to the orange juice, shook it up, and took a long gulp. He was trying to focus on work, but the only thing that was on his mind was Dana. He had a wonderful night with her, a night that he didn't want to end. Dana was everything that he wanted in a woman. She was funny, smart, and sexy all rolled into one. Stone was looking forward to spending more time with Dana. He was hoping this time they could go out on a real date. He pulled out his cell phone and was about to send Dana a text message when a call came over on his radio that an armor truck had just been robbed. Stone looked up at the street sign and saw that he wasn't too far from the location.

Stone put his phone away and headed straight towards the location. Even though they didn't say it over the radio, he had a feeling that it was the same team behind the bank robberies. *"Not on my watch,"* Stone said to himself. The dispatcher over the radio said that the gunmen fled in a black *Charger* and a black *Camaro*. Stone was just about to make a right at the corner when out of nowhere a black *Camaro* zoomed passed him.

"Here we go," Stone said to himself as he quickly busted a U-turn and fell in line directly behind the *Camaro*. In an attempt to not blow his cover, Stone made sure he stayed a few feet behind the *Camaro*. He thought, maybe the driver would lead him to the gunmen's

headquarters. Stone slowed down when he noticed the *Camaro* stop for a red light. He pulled up on the side of the *Camaro* and waited a second before looking over at the driver. The tint on the *Camaro* was too dark for Stone to see through.

Suddenly the driver's window rolled down and a man wearing a president George Bush mask stared back at Stone. George Bush quickly raised his arm and fired a shot at the detective's face before stomping down on the gas and leaving the detective in his sights.

9
SPEEDING

Randy stomped down on the gas pedal as the *Camaro* zoomed past the garage. "Fuck!"

"Where the fuck did that cop come from?" Ghost asked, looking back over his shoulder out the back window. "Try to lose him!"

Randy zoomed from lane to lane in an attempt to leave the detective in the dust. The *Camaro* roared as it picked up speed. Randy stomped down on the brakes and made a sharp right turn down a narrow one way street. The *Camaro* skidded but it stayed on course. Randy knew that the detective had called in for back up and that it was only a matter of time before the police set up road blocks and a helicopter got involved. The *Camaro* zoomed through the intersection, avoiding a collision by an inch or two. Car horns blared loudly as the *Camaro* sped away.

Ghost looked over his shoulder and noticed that the detective's car was still behind them. "This motherfucker is still behind us!"

"I'm trying to lose him!" Randy said looking down at the speedometer that read 115 mph.

"We gonna have to split up!" Ghost said as he slammed a fresh clip in the base of the M-16. "There's a subway station coming up in three blocks. Let me out right there," he said reaching back and grabbing one of the bags filled with money. "Listen, this cop can only go after one of us!" Ghost told Randy. "If he goes after me, then I want you to ditch this car at the next block and hop in a cab!"

"And if he goes after me?" Randy asked.

"If he goes after you then you're going to have to shoot it out!" Ghost said seriously. Each member of the team knew how serious the job was before trey agreed to it. Now it was time for one of them to show what they were made of.

The *Camaro* came to a dramatic skidded stop in front of the subway station.

"If you get caught you know the rules, keep your mouth shut!" Ghost instructed. "I love you!"

"I love you too!" Randy replied as he watched Ghost slide out the passenger seat and disappear down the subway steps.

Ghost ran down the stairs full speed, pushing people out of his way until he finally reached the bottom. The only thing on his mind was not going to jail. He ran, hopped the turnstile, and made his way towards the crowded platform. Immediately, people began to yell and scream when they saw a man in a mask carrying a big machine gun. Ghost was just about to remove his mask and throw his gun away hoping to maybe blend in with the crowd when out of nowhere a uniform cop stood in front of him.

Without warning Ghost raised the M-16 and opened fire on the officer. The bullets chopped the cop down as if he was made of paper.

10

CHOICES

S tone turned the corner just in time to see a man in an Obama mask flee from the getaway car and disappear down the subway stairs with an M-16 in his hand. He had to make a quick decision; he could go after either the Camaro, or the gunman in the Obama mask.

Shit!" Stone cursed as he stomped down on the brakes. He dashed out the driver seat and headed down the subway stairs in pursuit of the masked gunman. He figured a man with a machine gun out in the open, surrounded by hundreds of innocent people, was more of a danger than following the *Camaro*. Stone hopped the turnstile and made his way down to the crowded platform. He removed his 9mm from his waist holster and held it low behind his leg, as he walked not wanting to scare the everyday commuters. Stone's eyes scanned from left to right as he slowly snaked his way through all the people that awaited a train.

The sound of a machine gun being fired from the opposite direction grabbed Stone's attention, sending everyone who waited on the platform into a frenzy. As he headed towards where the gunshots came from, people were almost killing themselves to get as far away from the carnage as possible. Stone pushed his way through the crowd until he reached the officer that lay dead in a pool of his own blood.

"He went that way!" a blonde hair woman said, pointing down the dark tunnel.

Stone quickly hopped down, and onto the train tracks. In one hand, he held his 9mm and in the other his flash light. The small pebbles crunched with each step he took. Up ahead of him, Stone spotted a figure running. He quickly took off after the gunman. Stone put his head down and took off into sprint. He slowed down when he heard the sound of a shot being fired. Stone steadied his gun as he inched towards a door that rested in the cut. He looked down and saw a broken lock lying on the ground.

Stone took a step back, kicked the door open, and cautiously entered. In front of him stood, a pair of stairs followed by yet another door. Stone slowly descended the steps and pushed open the door. On the other side of the door was a smaller tunnel. The only difference was this tunnel had a stream of sewer water flowing through it, along with several rats that ran throughout the tunnel as if they owned it.

"Ah shit!" Stone cursed as he looked down at the nasty sewer water covering his fresh construction timberlands that he had just purchased about a week ago. The sound of water splashing grabbed Stone's attention.

He quickly followed the splashing sound. Stone turned the corner and froze when he looked down the barrel of an M-16.

"Drop that motherfucking gun!" Ghost growled as he pressed the barrel of the rifle into Stone's forehead. Having no other choice Stone did as he was told and tossed his 9mm down into the sewer water.

"Now toss your backup gun!"

"Listen, you don't want to do this," Stone said. "You're already in enough trouble, so killing a cop is the last thing you would want to do. Now why don't you put that gun down before somebody gets hurt?"

The man in the Obama mask didn't budge. "I'm going to count to three."

"I have a backup gun in the small of my back," Stone said. "I'm going to reach for it."

"Do it slowly!" Ghost warned. He wasn't taking any chances. One wrong move and he was sure to put a bullet right between the detective's eyes.

Stone slowly reached and removed his backup gun from the small of his back and tossed it down into the sewer water. In a blur, Stone came back up and grabbed the rifle. The M-16 went off as the two men fought for control of the gun. Stone kneed Ghost in his groin area forcing him to let go of the rifle, but before Stone had full control of the gun, Ghost landed a quick left followed by a right that stunned and dropped Stone off impact. While down in the sewer water, Stone felt around until he reached his 9mm. He rose up and opened fire on the fleeing target.

POW!

POW!

Stone quickly hopped back up to his feet and ran down the tunnel in search of the suspect, but stopped when he reached a fork in the tunnel. "Fuck!" he cursed loudly. He had no idea which way the suspect went and no longer having a flashlight would only make matters worse. After doing eeny, meeny, miny, moe in his head,

Stone decided to take the tunnel on the left. He jogged about a half a mile through the tunnel before finally giving up. He was so close to catching one of the violent bank robbers, but he let it slip through his fingers and to make matters worse, his clothes were ruined and smelled like a bowl of shit.

*****

Stone hopped back up onto the platform from the train tracks with a defeated look on his face. He knew he was so close to bringing down one of the violent bank robbers, but now he would have to start from scratch. He had fired several shots at the gunman and silently wondered if any of his bullets had found a home in the target.

"Detective, are you alright?" a uniform officer asked.

"I'm good," Stone said, as he walked pass the uniform officer and headed straight towards Captain Fisher.

"Stone please tell me that you got that bastard?" Captain Fisher asked and then frowned when he smelled Stone.

"Nah… Sorry captain, he got away," Stone answered. "What about the *Camaro*? Did y'all catch the driver?"

Captain Fisher shook his head no. "When they found the *Camaro* it was empty. I have a few of my men dusting it for prints now."

"I give you my word that I'm going to catch these animals," Stone promised. On the inside, he felt bad about letting the gunman get away, but something inside of him told him that he would definitely be running into the violent bank robber again.

"Stone you're one of my best men," Captain Fisher said seriously. "I know you did your best back there and that's all that matters." He patted Stone on the back.

"Now go home, get cleaned up and try to enjoy the rest of your night."

Stone climbed behind the wheel of his car and headed home to his apartment. Pictures of the gunman in the Bill Clinton mask kept replaying repeatedly in his head. In his mind, Stone saw all the mistakes he had made and vowed that the next time him and one of the gunmen crossed paths, the outcome would be different.

When Stone made it inside his apartment, the first thing he did was remove his stinking clothes and head straight to the kitchen, where he poured himself a drink. Stone downed the liquid fire in one gulp and then quickly refilled his glass. He looked over on the counter at his 9mm and a part of him felt like he had let everyone down by letting the gunman escape. The more Stone sipped his drink, the more his mind began to wonder and the more his mind wondered, the more he began to think about Dana. Right now, he could really use her company. Stone reached down in his pants pocket and found out that his phone was ruined. He finished his drink, jumped in the shower, and then headed out the door to get a new phone.

SILK WHITE

11
REGROUP

Dana paced back and forth in the dining room of the house where everyone was supposed to meet up. She looked around and saw Randy and Dougie sitting at the table with long worried looks on their faces. Everyone had made it back safely, everyone except Ghost. Dana had been at the house for over two hours waiting for Ghost to arrive. She didn't want to think the worst, but the more she paced the more she worried. Ghost was her big brother and just the thought of something bad happening to him had her ready to go crazy. "Ghost should have been here by now."

"Calm down," Randy said in a calm tone. "The rules are we wait six hours after a job before we do anything."

"You shouldn't have left him," Dana said staring at Randy. "The rules are we always stick together and work as a unit, not split up," she said with a cold edge in her voice.

"It was Ghost's idea that we split up in the first place," Randy matched Dana's tone. "We all knew the risk beforehand so let's not start to point fingers."

"Y'all two chill out," Dougie said speaking for the first time.

"Where did you leave Ghost?" Dana asked.

"I didn't, *"leave"* Ghost anywhere," Randy said defensively. "He, *"asked"* me to drop him off at the subway."

"Why the fuck would he say some shit like that? That don't even make no sense!" Dana fumed.

"It was this detective on our ass and this motherfucker came out of nowhere," Randy explained. "And Ghost thought it would be best if we split up. The shit happened so fast that the next thing I know, I saw Ghost hop out the car and disappear down the subway steps."

Just as Dana was about to respond, everyone at the table stopped when they heard the front door open and in walked Ghost.

"Oh my God! I was so worried!" Dana said, as she ran, jumped in her brother's arms, and tried to squeeze the life out of him. "Are you alright?" she asked as she began checking him for wounds.

"I'm good," Ghost smiled as he sat his bag of money down on the table. "That fucking detective almost had me," he admitted. "But I had to put the moves on his ass," he laughed.

"Celebration time!" Dougie announced walking from the kitchen with a bottle of champagne in each hand.

Ghost removed his soiled clothes and stood in his boxers. "I'd like to make a toast," he said getting everyone's attention. "At last we are finally free," he began. "We have successfully taken down enough banks to finally retire and ride off into the sunset. I want to thank every one of you because without each of you, none of this would have been possible. To happiness, power, and family," he said raising his glass and clanking it against all the other glasses. Ghost had been planning and preparing for this day for the last three years. His biggest fear was going broke, so he made sure he planned for anything and everything that could go wrong. Deep down inside, Ghost was happy to call it quits. Tonight, he came close to losing his life or spending the rest of it in a cage. Ghost loved money, but he also knew when it got too hot in the kitchen it was time to step out.

"I'm just happy you made it back in one piece," Dana smiled. Just the thought of losing Ghost made her stomach feel like she was on a roller coaster. Sure, they had their ups and downs like any other family, but at the end of the day, they loved each other and would always be there for one another. Now that she knew Ghost was good, Dana's train of thought shifted over to Stone. He had been heavily on her mind ever since the last time the two were in each other's presence. Dana's thoughts were interrupted when Ghost began to divide the money. As usual, he sat each member's share of money in front of him or her.

"Job well done," Ghost smiled. "In the next three weeks I'm out of here," he announced. "I'll be throwing a big going away party before I leave though."

"Out? What you mean you out? Where are you going?" Dana nosily asked.

Ghost sipped his drink slowly. "I'm moving to Hawaii."

"What's in Hawaii?" Dougie asked.

"A peace of mind," Ghost countered. New York had been good to him, but he wanted to go somewhere, where he could just kick his feet up and relax for once in his life.

"So you just going to leave us up here like this?" Randy asked with a bit of frustration in his voice.

Ghost looked at Randy as if he had lost his mind. "Leave y'all up here like what? We've all made well over two million dollars so nobody is stuck here. If you decide to remain here that's because you choose to be here."

"I didn't mean it like that," Randy said trying to downplay his frustration. "We like a family and if you leave, it's kind of like you breaking up the family."

"You all are more than welcome to come with me to Hawaii," Ghost offered. "Now if y'all will excuse me, I have to take a shower and get this stench off of me."

Once Ghost was gone, Randy spoke. "So the rest of you all are leaving too?"

Dougie shrugged and finished sipping on his drink. Randy then turned to Dana. "What about you Dana? You leaving too?"

"I'm not sure yet," she said honestly. Now that she had met Stone, she wasn't in a hurry to go anywhere, but in the back of her mind, Dana knew that Ghost would more than likely try to persuade her to go to Hawaii with him.

"You have been acting a little strange lately," Randy smiled. "You been getting some dick. I know that look anywhere. Who is he?"

"None of your business," Dana sucked her teeth. Randy laughed loudly. "You already know Ghost don't approve of any of the men you choose to date. Didn't he beat up your last two boyfriends?"

Dana was about to reply when her cell phone buzzed, *the perfect distraction,* she thought. She received a text message from a number she didn't recognize.

Unknown: hey this is Stone I lost my phone earlier so this is my new number...would you like to join me for dinner tonight?

Dana: I would love to

Dana got up and looked at Randy. "Who my new boyfriend is, is neither you nor Ghost's concern," and just like that she was gone.

12

BAD TIMING

After finishing two and a half bottles of champagne, Randy decided that it was time for him to call it a night. He got up, exited the house, and got in his car. He pulled out at a normal pace and cruised down the road. His car swerved a little, but for the most part, he felt that he was doing fine on the road. Randy's strong point was driving so he didn't having a problem while under the influence. As Randy drove, he began to think about his future. It wasn't until tonight when he heard Ghost's plan about moving to Hawaii that he began thinking about his own future. The truth was that Randy had never been outside of New York unless he and the team were on a job, but that didn't count. *"Fuck am I supposed to do when Ghost leaves?"* Randy said to himself. *"This nigga Ghost only ever cared about himself. He didn't even have the decency to check and see if the rest of the crew was good on money or how anyone else felt about him leaving."*

Randy had always been jealous of Ghost and felt that he always showed favoritism towards Dana because she was his sister. He felt that in Ghost's eyes, all he was, was a driver. Several times Randy begged Ghost to let him prove himself on a job, but every time Ghost dismissed the idea. "Fuck Ghost!" Randy blurted out. The sudden vibration of his cell phone vibrating on his hip caused him to take his eyes off the road for a second. Randy began reading the text message he received when his car began to sway over to the right onto the shoulder of the road. He quickly jerked the steering wheel to left and steadied the car. Twenty seconds later Randy noticed flashing lights in his rearview mirror.

"Fuck!" he cursed out loud. He looked over at the big bag of money that rested in the passenger seat along with the George Bush mask. *"Fuck that! I'm not going to jail,"* Randy said to himself as he grabbed the .38 that rested on his lap and pulled over to the side of the road. He quickly reached over, grabbed the George Bush mask, and tossed it into the backseat.

Randy watched nervously as the white officer stepped out of his car and hurried towards his car.

"Good evening!" the officer said in a stern, not-fucking-around tone. "License and registration, please!" Randy reached over in the glove compartment and handed the officer his license and registration card.

The officer looked over the license for a second and then said, "In a bit of a rush tonight?"

"Just a little tired, ready to get home," Randy flashed a phony smile.

"I noticed you ran off the road back there," the officer returned the phony smile. "You been drinking tonight?"

"No sir," Randy answered quickly.

"Be back in a second," the officer said and then headed back to his car.

Randy sat behind the wheel of his car as panic took over. He didn't like how the officer had looked at him and he was sure that he would look for any reason to arrest him. *"I wonder if he noticed the George Bush mask in the backseat or the bag full of money sitting over on the passenger seat?"* he thought out loud.

Seconds later Randy noticed a second police car pull up to the scene. He watched closely through his side view mirror as the two cops spoke amongst each other and then slowly made their way towards his car.

"Sir, would you mind stepping out of the car for a second?" the original officer asked in his usual stern tone.

"Why? Is there a problem officer?" Randy asked nervously. His nervousness was beginning to make the officers suspicious.

"Sir, step out of the vehicle please!" the original officer shouted with his hand positioned on his hip.

"Yes sir," Randy opened the door, faked like he was about to step out of the vehicle then quickly raised his gun, and shot the original officer in the face. He then turned and opened fire on the second officer. The second officer dived out of the line of fire just as the bullets whizzed pass his head.

Randy threw the gear in drive and gunned the engine. There was no way he was going to jail tonight. He kept his head ducked low as the sound of gunfire sounded off loudly behind him.

The second officer fired off six shots in a rapid succession. One of the bullets managed to hit the back tire of Randy's car. The second officer watched as the suspect's vehicle spun out of control and then finally crash into a light pole.

The crash left blood leaking from Randy's head. The impact from the collision caused his face to violently bounce off the steering wheel. Randy opened his door and was about to try and make a run for it, but thought otherwise when several cop cars surrounded his car with guns trained on him. Having no other choice, Randy dropped his weapon and surrendered.

13

IT TAKES TWO TO TANGO

Stone stepped a foot out of his building and spotted Dana's cocaine-white *Benz* coupe sitting curb side. He quickly walked over and slid in the passenger seat. Instantly the butter-soft leather massaged his back, making him feel right at home. "Nice to see you again," he said and then leaned over and kissed Dana on the cheek.

"Likewise," Dana smiled and pulled out into traffic. After the rough day that she and her crew had, seeing

Stone's face was like a breath of fresh air and she welcomed it with open arms. "So how was your day?"

"Rough," Stone admitted. "And honestly I don't really want to talk about work."

"Long day, huh?" Dana said placing her hand on Stone's thigh. "Don't worry, after tonight work will be the last thing on your mind."

"How was your day?"

"My day was pretty rough too," Dana answered. "But it just got better," she said flashing a sexy smile. When Dana was in Stone's presence, she felt like nothing else mattered or even existed.

The *Benz* pulled up in front of a fancy restaurant. Dana stepped out dressed in a tight fitting red dress with a high split on both sides. Her hair was in a high neat bun and a pair of diamond chandelier looking earrings hung from her lobes. On her feet, she wore a pair of expensive red pumps. She handed her keys to the valet parking attendant who stood out front.

"Scratch my car and I'm going to scratch your ass!" Dana said seriously, and then held out her arm. Stone intertwined his arm in hers as the two entered the restaurant. Stone stepped foot in the restaurant and immediately felt out of place. He looked around and saw several rich, white men dressed in tuxedos and expensive looking tailored suits. He looked down at his outfit and felt a little embarrassed. He had on a pair of soft bottom shoes, a pair of blue jeans, a collared shirt, and a dark colored blazer. Dana had told him to put on something nice because they were going to a nice restaurant, but he had no clue that they would be coming to such an exquisite establishment.

"Your name please?" the hostess asked politely.

"Wilford."

The hostess searched her book until she came across Dana's name. "Right this way," she smiled and led them through the restaurant over towards their table.

Stone felt the eyes of all the rich couples in the restaurant assaulting him as him and Dana walked past. Some even gave him and Dana dirty looks, but none were brave enough to say anything. The hostess led Dana and Stone over to a booth in the cut. She handed them both a menu and said, "Your waitress will be with you shortly," then turned and walked away.

The lights in the restaurant were dim and soft music played from the speakers at a low level, making the atmosphere feel even more romantic.

"So what do you think?" Dana flashed a bright smile.

"This place is magnificent," Stone replied. "But honestly I ain't even gonna front. I can't afford to take you to a place like this."

"You don't have to pay for anything tonight. I got it. All I need you to do is enjoy yourself and have a good time," Dana smiled. "There is nothing wrong with a woman treating her man from time to time."

"Keep treating me like this and I might get spoiled."

"Listen," Dana said seriously. "I don't want you worrying about money while you with me. I make more than enough money to take care of the both of us."

"It's just the man inside of me that wants to pay."

"The amount of money you have or make doesn't make you a man," Dana told him. "Now keep quiet and let me take care of my baby."

"Oh, I'm your baby now?"

"You think I would have given you all my goodies if you weren't," Dana seductively licked her lips.

After the two ordered their food, Stone sipped on his glass of red wine and admired Dana's beauty for a moment. It was rare to find a woman now days with brains and beauty. Stone tried to find something wrong with Dana, but came up empty. In his eyes, she was the perfect woman and the perfect distraction from work.

"What you over there thinking about?" Dana asked, snapping Stone out of his thoughts.

"You," Stone answered. "It's crazy when the person you been looking for all of your life is sitting directly across from you and you can actually touch her."

"And how are you so sure that I'm that girl?" Dana asked with a raised brow. "We haven't even known each other that long."

"When it's sitting in front of you, trust me, you know."

"What happens if you meet somebody better tomorrow?"

"Not happening," Stone said confidently and then took another sip of his wine. "Thank you again for taking me to such a nice restaurant."

"Boy hush," Dana said waving him off. "How would you feel about meeting my brother?" She came right out with it.

"I don't see that being a problem."

"He's supposed to be having this big party in a few weeks," Dana explained. "And I would like for you to meet him."

"What's the special occasion?" Stone asked.

"He's moving to Hawaii," Dana paused to take a sip of her wine. "My brother and I are really close and I think he's expecting me to go to Hawaii with him," she explained. "I think I'm going to tell him at the party that I won't be accompanying him."

"Do you want to go?" Stone asked. He really liked Dana, but if she really wanted to go to Hawaii with her brother, he wasn't about to stop her.

"Honestly?" Dana paused again. "Honestly I want to be with you and wherever you are," she looked Stone in his eyes. "A lot of people may think I'm moving too fast, but I just know what I want and what I want is you."

Her words caught Stone off guard. Truthfully, he felt the exact same way, but just didn't have the courage or the heart to say it. He leaned over the table and gave Dana a slow long drawn out kiss. "I would love to meet your brother at the party."

"Thank you so much," Dana smiled brightly. She knew that more than likely Ghost wouldn't approve of her and Stone's relationship, but she could tell by just looking in Stone's eyes that he had her back and would back her up and hold her down. Under the table, Dana removed her shoe, placed her foot directly on Stone's crotch, and began massaging his package with her foot. "I'm really not that hungry after all. Let's get out of here. I got a few things I want to do to you," she said in a sexually charged tone.

"I thought you would never ask," Stone smiled.

Dana paid the bill and left a hefty tip on the table and just like that, they were gone.

*****

Stone and Dana barely even made their way through the front door of Dana's baby mansion before their hands were all over each other. They kissed like newlyweds as they moved throughout the house removing each other's clothes. Stone looked at Dana standing there looking beautiful in nothing but a black laced thong and her red pumps and couldn't resist any longer. He walked over, ripped Dana's thong off like a savage, dropped down to his knees, and began kissing her thick thighs as if his life depended on it. Stone surprised Dana with his strength as he picked her up, flipped her upside down, put her legs around his neck, held her by her waist, and brought her dampness to his tongue. Stone gripped Dana while her moans rose and her hair dropped out of the neat bun and covered his toes. One by one, her high heels dropped from her feet. Dana grabbed Stone's dick and began to jerk it, while he ate her out. She took him deep inside her mouth, did that while he put his tongue inside her as deep as he could.

Stone's tongue made circles as he licked on her clit. He licked figure eights and gave her the sweetest torture.

Dana's head moved from side to side, jerked, and moaned as if the devil inside her was fighting for freedom.

"Oh my God! Put me down!" Dana begged. "I can't take it no more!"

Stone positioned Dana back right side up and carried her over to the counter. He gently sat Dana on the counter and entered her slowly as the two shared a long kiss.

"Fuck me Stone!" Dana growled in his ear. "Fuck me!" She squeezed Stone's ass forcing him to fuck her, forcing him to thrust even harder. She bit her bottom lip and watched Stone's tool move in and out of her warmth at a steady pace. "Ahh, ahhh, ahhh!" she moaned loudly. Dana threw her head back, closed her eyes tight, opened her mouth wide, and moved her head side to side, in pain and in pleasure. She was in heaven, but she was sweating as if she were in hell's kitchen.

Stone wrapped his hand around Dana's throat, as he plowed in and out of her sopping wet insides like a mad man.

"Stone! Stone! Oh my God, Stone! Shit!" Dana's legs trembled and then her entire body did the same.

Stone let out a strong roar as he shot his load and erupted inside of Dana.

"Oh shit!" Stone said out of breath as he walked over to the couch and flopped down lazily. Sex with Dana was an amazing experience, an experience he could see himself getting used to. Dana was beginning to make him nervous. He just couldn't find anything wrong with her. While Stone was deep in his thoughts, Dana disappeared upstairs.

Dana returned downstairs with a soapy washcloth in her hands. She cleaned Stone up so gently making sure not to miss a spot.

"Why are you so good to me?"

"You deserve the best and that's what I'm going to give you," Dana leaned forward and kissed Stone on the lips.

Stone was getting ready to respond, when he heard his cell phone ring. He looked down at his phone and saw that it was Captain Fisher. "Hold on baby, I have to take this," he said as he got up and walked out of ear shot so Dana couldn't hear his conversation. "Hey Captain," he answered.

"Get down to the station now. We have one of the gunmen from the bank robberies in custody!" Captain Fisher ended the call.

Stone walked back into the sitting room and took a minute to take in Dana's naked beauty for a moment. She was a beautiful woman and Stone considered himself lucky to have her in his life. "Baby I have to run out for a minute."

"Will you be coming back?" Dana asked, putting on her sad puppy face.

"It may be real late by the time I get done baby."

Dana got up and walked over to the counter where her purse rested. She reached down in her purse, removed her house key off the ring of keys, and handed it Stone. "I don't care how late it is, just come back." She grabbed the back of Stone's head and gave him a sloppy tongue kiss.

Stone looked down at the key in his hand and smiled. "Thanks baby I'll be back; gotta go," he said then disappeared out the door.

14

INVESTIGATION

Stone stepped foot in the precinct and noticed that it was full of commotion as usual. He was expecting to see cameras and reporters all over the place, but to his surprise, not one reporter or cameraman was present.

"Stone!" Captain Fisher called him over. "So glad you could finally join us," he said in a sarcastic tone of voice. "We got one of the bank robbers right in that room over there," Captain Fisher nodded towards a room down the hall. "We've kept this on the hush because I think you can make him talk. If he talks, we can bring down the entire organization." He cracked a smile. "If we would have announced his arrest to the world, the rest of his crew would have fled in fear that he had talked."

"So what do you need me to do?" Stone asked. He still had a little buzz from the wine that he and Dana had consumed earlier.

"I need you to go in there and make him talk," Captain Fisher stated plainly.

"I'm on it," Stone headed down the hall, but paused when he reached the door. He needed a second to gather his thoughts and gather his game plan together. He took a deep breath then entered the room. From the first glance at Randy, he didn't look like a bank robber. In fact, he looked more like a college student then a bank robber, but Stone had learned a long time ago not to judge a book by its cover.

"What's poppin?" Stone pulled a chair up to the table and sat down. "My man, check this out," he began. "I'mma keep it tall with you. You done got yourself in a fucked up situation," he paused to take in Randy's reaction. "We know that you are one of the bank robbers and now on top of that you shot a cop." Stone shook his head sadly. "I can help you, but I'm going to need you to help me."

Randy chuckled. "Help you how? I'm sure my picture is all over the news by now."

"No one knows about your arrest," Stone told him. "These are your two options. One you can tell me who your buddies are that helped you rob all these banks and walk away clean or two you cannot tell me anything and spend the rest of your life in jail. The choice is yours."

"And if I cooperate I get to walk away clean?" Randy asked with a raised brow.

Stone nodded his head yes.

"Fuck you! You just a worker! I need to hear that from your boss's mouth!" Randy said.

"I'll be back in a second," Stone said as he exited the room. He walked back into the other room where Captain

Fisher and a few other cops sat behind the two way mirror listening in on their conversation. "Captain I need you for a second."

When Stone and Captain Fisher were out the room, Stone spoke. "I need you to guarantee this scumbag something so he can give up his partners."

"I'm not guaranteeing this scumbag anything!" Captain Fisher barked. "Either he gives up his partners or he sits in jail forever! It's up to him!"

"Captain getting four violent bank robbers off the street is better than one," Stone pointed out. "It has to be something you can offer him."

Randy sat in the empty interrogation room with a nervous look on his face. He didn't want to roll over on Ghost and the rest of the crew, but for the last twenty minutes, he had been trying to convince himself that if they were in the same position that they would do the same thing. Not to mention Randy didn't like how Ghost had always played him like a sucker and made him drive all the time. In his mind he had no other choice than to do what he had to do and that was look out for himself.

Seconds later, the door opened and in walked Stone and Captain Fisher. "This here is my boss Captain Fisher," Stone said.

"Here are your options," Captain Fisher began. "One you can spend the rest of your life in jail. Two you can tell us who your partners are and serve eight years for your cooperation or you can take this last option." Captain Fisher paused for a second. "You can set up your partners. You can set up another bank robbery, we catch them red handed, and you get to walk away like nothing ever happened."

Stone could immediately see the wheels turning in Randy's head. Spend the rest of your life in jail or walk away free, was the decision that Randy had to make.

"So all I have to do is set up another bank robbery and y'all will be there to arrest my crew and I get to go free?"

Randy asked just making sure they all were on the same page. "I'm going to need that in writing captain."

"You can have that in writing, but did I mention that you only have two weeks to make this happen?" Captain Fisher smiled. "Now are you in or are you out?"

15
MAKE A CHOICE

Ghost pulled his black *Range Rover* in Dana's driveway and killed the engine. Several days passed since the last time he laid his eyes on his little sister, which was unusual since the two usually spoke every day. Lately, Ghost had noticed that Dana had been acting a little funny. Now he was here to see what was up. Ghost stepped out of the *Range Rover* in a slim fitting black tailored suit, with a pair of expensive hard bottom shoes on his feet. He rang the doorbell and waited patiently for a response. A few seconds later Dana answered the door in a short fitting silk red robe.

"Hey Ghost what you doing here?" Dana asked. Her brother just showing up at her house had caught her a little off guard.

"Expecting company?" Ghost asked, taking in the sexy getup that his sister wore.

"Actually I was," Dana said standing firm. Usually she tried to keep her boyfriends a secret, but not anymore.

"We need to talk," Ghost said, entering the house without bothering to wait for an invitation. "I got a few things I need to talk to you about." He made his way over to the bar area and poured himself a shot of Coconut 1800. Ghost downed the liquid fire in one gulp, and then quickly refilled his shot glass. "What's up with Hawaii?"

"What's up with it?" Dana asked with an attitude. She was tired of Ghost turning his dreams into *their* dreams.

"You began to pack your things and say your goodbyes yet?" Ghost asked.

"I'm not going to Hawaii Ghost."

"Fuck you mean you not going?" Ghost downed another drink then looked at his little sister as if she was insane.

"I said I'm not going," Dana said with her arms folded across her chest. "I'm going to stay here with my new boyfriend."

"Your new boyfriend?" Ghost echoed with his face crumbled up. "How long have you been knowing this guy for?"

"A few weeks."

"You don't even know him; my point exactly!" Ghost shouted. "I've worked my ass off so we could be straight and be able to live with our feet kicked up on an island somewhere!"

"I can still live with my feet kicked up without going to Hawaii," Dana said defensively. "I'm staying here and that's final."

"If you stay, there's always a chance that the cops may figure out our identity later on down the line and come get you," Ghost explained. "I know you think I don't want to see you happy, but that's the furthest from the truth. My main priority is to keep you safe!"

"Ghost I don't know if you've noticed or not, but I'm grown and well capable of taking care of myself."

Ghost laughed. He hated that his sister was so stubborn. If she stopped being so defensive all the time, she would clearly see that he was only trying to look out for her. "When can I meet him?"

"Huh?"

"When can I meet him?" Ghost repeated. "Your new boyfriend."

"I'll bring him to *your* going away party," Dana replied.

"Listen Dana," Ghost said walking up on Dana. "I know you are grown and I'm going to respect your wishes, but please know that I'm only trying to look out for you like I've always done since we were kids."

"I understand, but I'm not a kid anymore Ghost," Dana said. "I'm grown now and I know I'm your little sister, but you are going to have to start treating me like a grown woman."

"You got it," Ghost smiled. "From now on I'll treat you like a grown woman and let you make your own decisions."

"And promise me you'll be nice when I bring my boyfriend to the party," Dana said, giving Ghost a stern look.

"I'll see what I can do," Ghost smiled as he headed for the door.

"Where you going?"

"Randy just text me asking me to meet him at his crib," Ghost replied. "I've been watching the news. The cops still have no clue who we are, but I still want you to fly under the radar. You know the rules, stay low key and don't make any big purchases."

"You already know," Dana said, tightly hugging her brother.

She watched him climb back in his *Range Rover* and pull out into traffic.

16

I SEE YOU

S tone sat in the back of a van, alongside a young detective that was there holding a camera. He'd gotten a call from Randy informing him that the leader of the bank robbing crew, a man they called Ghost, agreed to meet him at his apartment today in about five minutes. Randy had described Ghost as a handsome, tall man that would be dressed in a nice suit.

"So what have you heard about this Ghost guy?" the detective that held the camera asked.

"I haven't heard too much about him," Stone shrugged. "All I know is that he's an animal and a violent man that needs to be off the streets."

"Why can't we arrest this guy today?"

"Because we need Randy to get this guy to agree to do another bank job, so that we can catch him and the rest of his team red handed," Stone explained.

"Hold on, I think we got some action!" the detective with the camera said. Stone looked up and noticed a black Range Rover pull up to the curb. A minute later, a man stepped out in a black slim fitted *Armani* suit. Just from how the man walked, Stone knew from first look that this was his man. That was indeed the man they called, Ghost.

"That's him," Stone whispered as the detective next to him snapped several pictures of Ghost heading into the building. Once Ghost disappeared inside the building, Stone and the detective quickly moved to the back of the van and covered their ears with headphones, hopping that Randy could get Ghost to incriminate himself on the wire.

17

SWITCHING SIDES

Randy looked at his reflection in the mirror for the hundredth time. He was afraid that Ghost would be able to tell that he wore a wire. A part of Randy felt bad about setting up his crew. They had all known each other for over fifteen years, which is what made his decision even more difficult. Randy had been convincing himself for the past few days that Ghost only cared about Ghost and if the shoe were on the other foot; he would have done the same exact thing. *"Fuck that it's either them or you,"* Randy told himself. Not to mention Randy had blew most of his money anyway, so the deal that the cops offered him would be like a new start for him to get his life together. A strong knock at the door snapped Randy out of his zone. "I'm coming!" he yelled, gave himself a once over, then headed to the door. "Glad you could make it Ghost." Randy stepped to the side so that Ghost could enter.

Ghost stepped inside the small apartment, looked around, and then frowned. "What did you do with all of your money?" He shook his head.

Randy walked into the kitchen area then returned carrying two drinks in his hands. "Ghost I need your help," he said in a serious tone. "I got robbed the other night."

"Got robbed?" Ghost echoed. For all the years, he'd known Randy, he'd never been the type to get robbed. "When did this happen?"

"Two days ago."

"Why didn't you come to me when it happened?" Ghost asked.

"I was trying to figure out something on my own," Randy replied. "Plus I was embarrassed and you know men like us are not supposed to get robbed."

"So what do you need from me?"

"I'm a little short on cash." Randy's eyes diverted down to the floor. "So I was wondering if we could maybe hit another bank."

Ghost chuckled. "Randy if you're asking me to rob a bank then the answer is no." Ghost was discipline enough to never talk reckless, especially not in his own place. "If you need some cash then I can help you out."

"I know you getting ready to move and everything so I didn't want to ask you for no money."

"So you rather ask me to rob a bank?" Ghost gave him a suspicious look. If he hadn't been dealing with Randy for over fifteen years, he might have thought something was up, but since it was Randy, so he looked past it.

"Listen Randy if you're strapped for cash, I'll help you out. We are like family and family always supposed to look out for family."

As soon as the words left Ghost lips, Randy immediately felt like a piece of shit for even agreeing to set his crew up and hang them out to dry, but now he was at the point of no return. Even if he wanted to back out of the deal, it was too late. "You sure that won't be too much on you with you leaving and all?"

"It's never too much for family," Ghost said finishing his drink and standing up. "I'll have something for you when you come to my party next week."

"I really appreciate this," Randy replied. "Anything you need me to do for you?"

"All I need you to do is to take care of yourself when I leave and looked after my sister while I'm gone."

"I thought she was going with you."

Ghost sighed. "She's her own woman and she said she's staying here."

"You going to let her?"

Ghost nodded his head. "It's time for her to grow up. I'm out so if you need me you know how to reach me." He stopped at the door and turned around. "And I know you didn't get robbed for all your money. You back gambling again aren't you?"

Randy nodded his head yes. "I'm sorry Ghost."

"Did you really get robbed?" Ghost asked.

"No I lost all of my money gambling," Randy admitted. He had actually lost most of his money gambling; not to mention the money that the police had taken from him. He figured that Ghost didn't really buy his getting robbed story so he decided to be honest.

"I'll have something for you when you come to the party next week," Ghost said and then made his exit.

Once Ghost was gone, Randy quickly snatched the wire from his chest and tossed it to the ground. "Fuck!" he cursed loudly. That was too close of a call for his liking. If Ghost found out that he was wearing a wire, he could only imagine what Ghost would have done to him. Randy quickly pulled out his cell phone and called Stone.

"We need more," Stone answered.

"What you mean you need more?" Randy snapped.

"He didn't admit to robbing no banks and he didn't agree to rob another bank with you. We have nothing on him," Stone told him. "If you want to walk, then you better give me something that I can work with."

Randy hung up with a frustrated look on his face. *"Fuck this shit! Whatever money Ghost gives me next week I'm just going to use that money and go on the run,"* he told himself. He knew there was no way that Ghost would agree to rob another bank. Ghost was out and once Ghost's mind was made up, it wasn't no changing it. Randy grabbed a bottle of liquor, turned the bottle up and guzzled the liquid fire as if it was water. He had to figure something out and figure it out fast.

18
IT JUST GOT REAL

G host stepped out of his *Range Rover* and entered the fancy building where his lawyer's office was held. On the ride over, Ghost's mind was stuck on him and Randy's conversation. He had never heard such a bullshit story in his life, but since he didn't know what Randy was up to, he decided to play along. Randy had been known for being a notorious gambler so Ghost just figure he gambled most of his money away like he'd done in the past. Ghost's plan was to give Randy $250,000 and then disappear to Hawaii and never be seen or heard from again.

"Hey, how are you doing Jessica? Can you tell Mr. Goldberg that I'm here to see him please?" Ghost asked, smiling at the receptionist.

"Sure thing Mr. Ghost." Jessica picked up her phone, pressed one button on the speed dial, spoke to the person on the other end, and then hung up. "Mr. Goldberg is expecting you," she told Ghost.

"Thank you," Ghost said and then headed to the office that rested at the end of the hall. He entered the office and spotted his lawyer.

Mr. Goldberg sat, leaned back with his feet kicked up on his desk, and a cigar in his mouth. "Good to see you again Ghost," Mr. Goldberg said smiling as he got up and shook Ghost's hand. "How can I help you today?"

"As you know, recently I invested some money with Brent Harrington's company," Ghost said. "I need you to call his office and let him know that I may need to take $250,000 from what I invested."

"What's wrong Ghost; money getting tight?" Mr. Goldberg asked. For as long as he knew Ghost, he knew the man was well organized and always thought three steps ahead of everybody else.

"No it's not me. I'm just trying to help out a good friend of mines."

"Be careful Ghost. Friends and family have been known to stab people in the back faster than strangers," Mr. Goldberg said as he picked up his phone and dialed Brent's number.

Ghost sat back and began to think about Dana and her new boyfriend. When the confused look that Mr. Goldberg had on his face, it grabbed his attention. "What's wrong?"

"It says that Brent's number has been disconnected," Mr. Goldberg said. He tried the number again, and shook his head. "The number has been disconnected. Do you have another number I can reach him at?"

"No," Ghost said shamefully.

"I'll check his website." Mr. Goldberg tapped a few keys on his keyboard and shook his head with a disgusted look on his face. "His website has been taken down as well."

"Tell me this is a joke," Ghost said seriously.

"I'm afraid not," Mr. Goldberg replied. "How much money did you invest with this dirt bag?"

"Two million."

Mr. Goldberg whistled. "Damn that's a lot of money. I hate to say this, but I think your friend Brent Harrington ran a scam on you."

"No this can't be happening," Ghost said shaking his head. He had invested his entire life savings with Brent. All the money that he had risked him and his sister's lives was down the drain. Now it all felt like a bad dream, but unfortunately for Ghost, this wasn't a dream. It was reality. "That was all of my money."

"Ghost if you need it, I can loan you $10, 000," Mr. Goldberg offered.

"Nah I'm good. I'll call you in a couple of days." Ghost stood to his feet and then made his exit.

Ghost slid behind the wheel of his *Range Rover* and banged on the steering wheel as he cried his eyes out. The feeling of losing all of his money had completely broken him down to the point of no return. "What the fuck am I supposed to do now?" he asked out loud. Ghost was mad at himself for being stupid enough to trust Brent. He didn't know what he was going to do, but what he did know was that something definitely had to be done.

19

IS IT REAL

"**D**o you love me?" Dana asked, taking a sip from her glass of wine. Her and Stone had spent the entire night making love and now they were sitting, relaxing in Dana's hot tub getting their thoughts together.

"Of course I do," Stone replied as he slowly gave Dana's foot a strong handed massage. The two of them were really getting hot and heavy for one another and neither cared what anybody thought about it.

"I had a long talk with my brother."

"Oh yeah?" Stone asked. "How did that go?"

"Better than I thought," Dana smiled. "He's starting to accept me as a woman and not just his baby sister anymore."

"Did you tell him that you weren't going to Hawaii with him?"

"Yeah I told him." Dana took a sip from her glass. "At first he wasn't really feeling it, but the more we spoke, the more he began to accept it."

While Dana spoke, Stone's mind was elsewhere. Visuals of the man they called Ghost popped up in his head repeatedly. He couldn't wait until it was time to arrest the mastermind behind all of the bank robberies. He hoped and prayed that Randy would come through with his promise and convince Ghost and his crew to try and take down another bank.

Once the two were out of the tub, Stone checked his phone to see if he had any missed calls or messages. When he turned back around, he saw Dana standing behind him with her hands hid behind her back and a smile on her face. "Close your eyes. I have a surprise for you," she told him.

"Huh?"

"Close your eyes baby," Dana said excitedly.

Stone closed his eyes and waited until Dana told him he could open them. Stone opened his eyes and saw a beautiful diamond studded *Rolex* sitting in a box.

"Surprise!" Dana shouted extending the box towards Stone.

Stone looked down at the diamond watch with a shocked look on his face. The watch was beautiful and from the looks of it, very expensive. "I can't accept this." He held the box back towards Dana.

"It's a gift from me to you," Dana smiled. "You are my man now and my man wears nothing but the best or nothing at all."

"This watch had to have cost you a small fortune," Stone said as he slid the watch down on his wrist and watched as the diamonds danced in the light.

"Money is no object when it comes to you," Dana said. She had saved most of her money from the bank jobs so she wouldn't lose any sleep over the money she spent on the watch. The truth was, she loved Stone, and would do just about anything to keep him happy.

"You sure you can afford this baby?"

"Stop worrying about money baby," Dana laughed. "I got us."

Stone was about to reply when he heard his cell phone ring. He looked down at the screen and saw Captain Fisher's name flashing across the screen. "Hold on baby, I have to take this." He walked off and answered his phone. "Yeah."

"Randy is about to try and meet with another member of the bank robbery crew so we can put a face to everyone. You might want to get down here quick," Fisher said and then ended the call.

Stone turned around and saw Dana looking at him with an upset look on her face.

"You have to go don't you?" she asked in a voice barely above a whisper.

"Yes baby but I won't be back too late," Stone promised.

The ringing of Dana's phone grabbed her attention. She looked down at her phone and saw Randy's name dancing across the screen. She quickly hit ignore and turned her attention back to Stone. "Baby can't you just stay for a little while longer?" she whined.

"I can't baby," Stone said, pulling Dana in close for a hug. "I'll try to be back in three hours tops." He kissed Dana on her forehead and then made his exit.

Dana stood there naked with a sad look on her face when her cell phone rang again. She was getting ready to hit ignore again, but paused when she saw Ghost's name on her screen. "Hello?"

"You busy right now?"

"Not really. Why? What's up?"

"Meet me at my crib in an hour," Ghost said and then ended the call.

20
PRESSURE BUST PIPES

"Testing... Testing... Can you hear me?" Randy said, speaking down into his chest.

"Yeah we can hear you loud and clear," Stone replied. "Now get in there and get us something we can use."

The driver pulled over about four blocks away from the house Randy was headed to and let him out.

Randy hopped out the back of the van and suspiciously looked over both shoulders as he headed towards the house. He hated to have to hang his friends out to dry, but now his back was against the wall and he felt as if he had no other choice. Randy reached the front of the fairly large house and rang the doorbell. Seconds later a dark skinned woman with a pregnant belly answered the door. "Hey Randy. What are you doing here?"

"Hey Cindy sorry for just popping up like this," Randy smiled. "Is your husband home? I really need to speak to him."

"Yeah, come on in," Cindy said stepping to the side so Randy could enter. "Dougie's in the house somewhere. Make yourself at home while I go find him."

Randy walked over to the living room and helped himself to a seat on the couch. He could hear another child upstairs playing. The longer he sat on that couch, the guiltier he felt. Seconds later Dougie came downstairs with a confused look on his face.

"Fuck you doing at my house?" Dougie spat.

"I need to talk to you about something. It's an emergency," Randy told him.

Dougie quickly led Randy out to the garage so they could have some privacy. "You know the rules. You never show up to no one's house; period!"

"I know, but I needs to talk to you."

"Okay so you call and we meet at the meeting crib like we always do!" Dougie lightly scolded.

"Listen Dougie, I'm fucked up right now and I need your help," Randy said in a desperate tone. "I fucked up and lost all my money."

"I know you not still out gambling all your money away?" Dougie growled. "When are you going to start using your head?"

"Listen, I don't want to hear no lecture. I need your help. Now are you going to help me or not?" Randy asked.

"What do you need?"

"I need you to help me convince Ghost to take down another bank."

Dougie gave Randy a sad look. "Are you serious? You can't be serious right now."

"Dougie I need you; please," Randy begged.

"First of all you know just as I know that Ghost ain't going to agree to no shit like that," Dougie said. "He's leaving next week. He'd never risk that just to hit another bank."

"That's why I need you to help me convince Ghost," Randy begged. "I really need the money man."

"I got about $50,000 you can have if you need it," Dougie offered.

"I'm not looking for no handout," Randy spat. "You know I work for mines."

"Listen, I'll run it by Ghost and see what he says, but if I were you, I wouldn't get my hopes up," Dougie told him.

"You're a life saver." Randy hugged Dougie.

"I have a question?" Dougie said. "How the fuck do you gamble away over two million dollars?"

Randy shrugged. "I don't know. It kind of just happened."

"You gonna have to stop that silly shit," Dougie said. Randy nodded his head pretending as if he agreed. "I appreciate you. Call me when you speak to Ghost."

"I got you," Dougie said as he watched Randy exit through the garage. He didn't know what was going on, but something about Randy didn't feel right. He didn't know what it was, but he was sure to get to the bottom of it.

21
WHAT'S GOING ON?

Dana pulled up to Ghost's house and killed the engine. She was curious to find out what was so important that Ghost needed her to come over right away. The first thing that came to her mind was maybe the cops had somehow found out their true identity, but she quickly scratched that idea because if that was the case, then Ghost definitely wouldn't have called a meeting at his house. Dana stepped out of the car and hurried to the front door where she rang the doorbell. Seconds later,

Ghost answered the door with a serious, no nonsense look on his face. The first thing Dana noticed was that Ghost wasn't wearing one of his expensive tailor made suits. Instead, he wore black jeans, a black thermal shirt, and a pair of black, steel toe boots.

"Hey," Dana said as she stepped inside the house. "Is everything alright?"

"I have to go to Los Angeles tonight," Ghost said. "If you don't hear from me in 48 hours, I want you and your new boyfriend to leave town. You got it?"

"Why? What's going on?"

"Listen to me Dana. I need you to do what I asked you to do. I don't have time to answer your questions right now," Ghost barked. "Now come on, I need you to drive me to the airport."

The ride to the airport was a quiet one. Dana wasn't quite sure what was going on, but she knew better than to continue asking. All she knew was that whatever was going on was serious. She knew Ghost well and when he was quiet like this, that usually meant that somebody was going to die. All Dana could do now was pray that her brother would make it back from Los Angeles in one piece.

Dana pulled into the drop off area at the airport. "Be careful and call me as soon as you can."

"I got you," was all Ghost said before exiting the car and heading inside the airport.

*****

Ghost boarded the plane and took his seat. The only thing on his mind was killing Brent. He still couldn't believe that he had let Brent trick him into giving him all of his hard earned cash. Brent had robbed Ghost without a gun and now he had to pay for his actions. During the plane ride, all Ghost could think about was how many other people Brent may have conned out of millions.

"You done fucked with the wrong one this time," Ghost said to himself. Thoughts of violence and horrible acts ran through his head for the entire plane ride. The streets gave Ghost his name because he was known for always flying under the radar and not being on Front Street. Being a flashy show off was never his thing. If the spot light were on him, he would always head in the other direction. That strategy had worked for him for years, but tonight. Brent had awaken a sleeping giant.

Ghost walked through the airport at a quick pace. He came here to handle business and that's all that was on his mind. He walked out of the airport and slid into the back seat of an *Escalade* that was parked curbside waiting for his arrival. The driver of the *Escalade* was an old friend of Ghost's who went by the name, Big T. Back in the day, Big T used to be Ghost's right hand man until a four year prison bid slowed him down.

"Everything you need is in that bag," Big T said and then pulled away from the curb out into traffic.

Ghost opened the black duffle bag that sat on the seat next to him. Inside he found a 9mm with a silencer attached to the barrel, along with two extra clips, and a black ski mask. Ghost rested his head back against the head rest and closed his eyes. His mind was moving a thousand miles per second and he took this time to rest his brain for a minute.

Big T pulled up onto the big estate over in the cut, not to draw too much attention to them. He placed the gear in park. "Time to roll."

Ghost rolled the ski mask down over his face, grabbed his gun, and quickly stepped out of the *Escalade*. He made his way over to the front door and shot the lock off. The shot was muffled and sounded like someone had pressed a key on an old type writer. Ghost entered the huge mansion with fire dancing in his eyes. He was on a mission and refused to be denied. Ghost tipped down the long elementary school like hallway. The further he walked, the louder voices could be heard. From the sound of it, it sounded like Brent and his family were having dinner or some kind of get together.

*****

Brent sat at the dining room table alongside his wife and business partner, an older man that went by the name of Sal. Brent's personal chef served them porterhouse steaks with a bake potato and vegetables on the side.

"Any new clients?" Sal asked raising his glass of wine to his lips. He and Brent had been getting rich off of others hard work for so long that they had forgotten what they were doing was wrong.

"I'm working on these two new guys looking to invest some big money. If all goes well I should be able to reel them in by the end of the week," Brent boasted. For him, his thrill came from outsmarting his clients. He loved to feel like he was the smartest person in the room. "By the end of the month, we should pull in another fourteen million."

"That's great," Ghost said stepping out from the shadows with a big gun in his hand. He snatched the ski mask off so Brent could see his face and know who was going to take his life. "I'll take my two million plus interest now if you don't mind."

"Gh… Gh… Ghost, hey man," Brent stuttered. "What are you doing here?"

"I tried calling your cell phone and your office and got no answer," Ghost said. "So I figured I'd drop by in person." He pulled out a chair and joined them at the table.

"Ghost, I was going to call you first thing in the morning and give you all my new numbers," Brent lied with a straight face. He was trying to keep cool and not show the fear that was inside of him. "Me and my partner Sal over here were just talking about you."

"Is that right?"

"Yes. We were saying how smart it was of you to invest with us and that in the next two years your money..."

"Cut the shit!" Ghost snapped cutting him off. "My money, I want it now! All of it!"

"I'm going to need some time Ghost," Brent told him. "Things like this, take time."

Ghost turned his gun on Sal and shot him out of his chair. Brent and his wife looked on in horror. The scene was so graphic that Brent's wife leaned over and threw up her meal.

Ghost then turned his gun on Brent's wife. "I need my money and I'm not going to ask you again."

"I have $30,000 upstairs in my safe; that's all I have," Brent said raising his hands in surrender. "Take it, it's yours."

"$30,000?" Ghost repeated. "Motherfucker where's my two million?"

"I don't have it. I used your money to make me more money and now all the money is currently tied up," Brent explained.

Ghost gave Brent a sad look and blew his wife's brains out right in front of him. Brent watched as his wife's body slid out of the chair and down to the floor as warm blood splashed across his face. Ghost roughly grabbed Brent by the back of his neck and forced him upstairs. The fact that Brent didn't have his money only pissed Ghost off even more. Ghost spun Brent around and slapped him across the face with his gun. Brent's head violently bounced off the wall before he crumbled down to the floor in a fetal position.

"Please don't kill me! I'm so sorry! I swear I'll get you your money back," Brent pleaded.

"How you gonna get my money back, huh? How?" Ghost barked as he cracked Brent over the top of his head with the gun opening up a huge gash. "You like to steal from people right? You like to rob people without a gun right?" Ghost blacked out and hit Brent repeatedly in the face with the gun until he was no longer recognizable. "Get your punk ass up!" He roughly snatched Brent up to his feet and shoved him towards the safe. "You have ten seconds to open that safe or I'm going to blow your brains all over that wall," Ghost said in a stern tone as he began to count.

Brent wiped blood from his eyes and slowly began to punch in the combination to the wall safe. Now he was willing to do whatever it took to get Ghost to stop hitting him. "Here it's open."

Ghost quickly moved towards the safe, removed the $30,000, and then turned his attention back on Brent. "Look at me you piece of shit!"

Brent looked up at Ghost from his knees. His eyes were begging Ghost not to kill him. The last thing he ever expected was for him to come back to his home blasting.

Once Brent looked at Ghost, he fired four shots into Brent's chest. Then he stood over him and put a bullet right between his eyes. Ghost then walked out the front door as if nothing never happened and slid back in the backseat of the *Escalade*.

Once Ghost was back in the truck; Big T smoothly pulled off the property and backed out into traffic. It was an unspoken rule not to talk after a job, so the two men rode in silence all the way back to the airport.

Thirty minutes later Big T pulled into the drop off area of the airport.

"Thanks for everything," Ghost said dropping $15,000 onto Big T's lap. "I appreciate it. I'll hit you when I touch down so you'll know I'm safe." Ghost stepped out the backseat and entered the airport never looking back.

22
I NEED YOU

When Ghost made it back to New York, the first thing he did was drop by Dana's house. On the plane ride, he had done a lot of thinking and he wanted to ask his sister's opinion on what he was thinking. Ghost slid out the backseat of the yellow cab, walked up to Dana's door, and rang the doorbell. Seconds later Dana opened the door with a big smile on her face.

Dana hugged Ghost tightly. "I'm so glad you made it back safely. Now get in here and tell me what's going on."

Ghost headed straight for the bar and poured himself a drink. "I lost all my money," he came straight out and said it. "I invested all my money with some conman out in Los Angeles and he fucked me over."

"He conned you out of all of your money?" Dana asked with a shocked look on her face. "Well I guess your trip to Hawaii is off now," she said sadly.

"No, I'm still going to Hawaii." Ghost paused for a second. "I was thinking about robbing another bank."

"No," Dana said quickly. "You said we were out, especially after how the last job almost cost you your life."

"I have no other choice."

"Yes you do. If you need money I'll be more than happy to give you half of my money," Dana said. "I have close to two million dollars and I'll split it with you."

"Thanks Dana but I can't take your money." Ghost downed his drink and quickly poured himself another. "This one last job and we're done."

"This isn't smart Ghost," Dana said, shaking her head. "I don't have a good feeling about this."

"Plus Randy fucked up his money gambling again and I promised to give him a couple of dollars," Ghost told her.

Dana sucked her teeth. "Ghost you can't keep on bailing Randy out every time he messes up his money."

"Dana I really need your help," Ghost said seriously. "This one last time, this one last bank, are you in or not?"

Dana stood there for a second giving the idea some thought and then she finally said, "I'm in." As soon as the words left her lips, she knew she was making a big mistake. Something about this job just didn't feel right. This job felt forced and rushed and their crew didn't work like that. Now that Dana had Stone in her life, nothing else really seemed to matter. The last thing she wanted to do was to get caught robbing a bank just when her life was beginning to change for the better. Dana watched as

Ghost made his exit and all she could do was wonder if she was making the right choice or not.

23

LIFE OF THE
PARTY

Dana pulled her *Benz* up in front of Ghost's house and killed the engine. She looked over at Stone and could immediately feel the butterflies in her stomach. She was nervous about him meeting Ghost. She knew that Ghost could be kind of intimidating at times and she didn't want Stone to feel uncomfortable.

"You alright?"

"Yeah baby, just thinking about a lot," Dana said.

"Wanna talk about it?"

"We can talk about it later." Dana put on a phony smile, stepped out of the car, and led Stone towards the front door. From all the cars that were parked out front, Dana could tell that the house was probably packed. For the past few days, the talk that Dana had with Ghost about taking down another bank had been haunting her.

Dana and Stone stepped foot in the house and the first thing they saw were people everywhere who looked to be having a good time. Young Jeezy's voice boomed through the speakers at a loud volume.

Stone looked around and saw strippers scattered around the house. Him and Dana quickly made their way over to the bar area and helped themselves to a drink. Stone took a sip of his drink and was about to say something to Dana, when he saw Randy walking around the house. *"What is he doing here? He better not blow me up in front of Dana,"* he thought to himself as Randy walked up.

"Hey Randy I want you to meet somebody," Dana said with an excited look on her face. "Randy meet my new boyfriend Stone and Stone meet my friend Randy," she said introducing the two.

"Nice to meet you Stone," Randy said acting as if this was his first time meeting Stone. "How did you two love birds meet?"

"We met at a lounge," Dana said, smiling from ear to ear.

"How sweet," Randy said in a phony tone. "Have you introduced him to your brother Ghost yet?"

"Not yet. I'm a little nervous," Dana said honestly. The reason she was so nervous was because she had never went against her brother in her entire life, but if for some reason he didn't like or approve of Stone, this would be her first time.

"Well it was nice to meet you Stone," Randy said and then walked off.

slammed the door behind him. "What the fuck are you thinking?" he barked.

"I'm sick and tired of this shit!" Dana snapped. "I love him and that's final! I don't care whether you like him or not! I love him and that's all that matters!"

"He's a cop Dana!" Ghost told her. "That's the cop that chased me down into the sewer and tried to blow my fucking head off!"

Dana took a second to process what Ghost had just told her and immediately felt like someone had knocked the wind out of her. *"There is no way that Stone is a cop. He dresses like a street guy and cops don't dress like that,"* Dana said to herself trying to convince herself. "Are you sure about this Ghost? Maybe you didn't get a good look at the cop's face in that dark sewer."

Ghost gave Dana a sad look. "Dana it's him," he told her.

"So he knows who you are?"

Stone's heart broke when he found out that Dana's brother was none other than Ghost. He knew that sooner or later he was going to have to tell her what he did for a living and that her brother was one of his main targets. Stone's thoughts were interrupted when Ghost walked up.

"I have somebody I want you to meet," Dana said smiling from ear to ear. "This is my boyfriend Stone and Stone this is my brother Ghost."

As soon as Ghost locked eyes on Stone, his jaw immediately went tight. He remembered Stone as the detective that chased him into the sewer and tried to lock him away for the rest of his life.

"Nice to meet you," Stone extended his hand.

Ghost looked down at his hand as if it had just been removed from the toilet and then turned his attention to Dana. "Can I have a word with you for a second?" He roughly grabbed Dana by the arm and escorted her upstairs to his bedroom. Ghost entered the bedroom and

"We can talk about it later." Dana put on a phony smile, stepped out of the car, and led Stone towards the front door. From all the cars that were parked out front, Dana could tell that the house was probably packed. For the past few days, the talk that Dana had with Ghost about taking down another bank had been haunting her.

Dana and Stone stepped foot in the house and the first thing they saw were people everywhere who looked to be having a good time. Young Jeezy's voice boomed through the speakers at a loud volume.

Stone looked around and saw strippers scattered around the house. Him and Dana quickly made their way over to the bar area and helped themselves to a drink. Stone took a sip of his drink and was about to say something to Dana, when he saw Randy walking around the house. *"What is he doing here? He better not blow me up in front of Dana,"* he thought to himself as Randy walked up.

"Hey Randy I want you to meet somebody," Dana said with an excited look on her face. "Randy meet my new boyfriend Stone and Stone meet my friend Randy," she said introducing the two.

"Nice to meet you Stone," Randy said acting as if this was his first time meeting Stone. "How did you two love birds meet?"

"We met at a lounge," Dana said, smiling from ear to ear.

"How sweet," Randy said in a phony tone. "Have you introduced him to your brother Ghost yet?"

"Not yet. I'm a little nervous," Dana said honestly. The reason she was so nervous was because she had never went against her brother in her entire life, but if for some reason he didn't like or approve of Stone, this would be her first time.

"Well it was nice to meet you Stone," Randy said and then walked off.

"No, I saw his face. He didn't see mines. I had on my mask," Ghost signed loudly. "You didn't tell him anything about what we do for a living, did you?"

"Never," Dana answered quickly.

"You in love with this guy, but you don't know what he does for a living?" Ghost asked.

Dana shook her head no. "I never asked."

"Do you know his middle name? Do you know his favorite color? Do you know his favorite food? What's his mother's name?" Ghost asked. "How the fuck are you in love with somebody who you know nothing about?"

Dana just stood there with a stupid look on her face. She was more hurt than embarrassed. In her line of work, speaking to or being associated with the police was a no-no. She knew right then that she had to break things off with Stone immediately.

"That's why I'm always so protective over you because I don't want to see you get hurt," Ghost said. "I know he's probably a nice guy and all, but when he finds out what you do for a living what do you think he's going to do? Marry you? No he's going to put a bullet in your head or either put you in jail for the rest of your life!"

"I have to kill him," Dana whispered as tears fell from her eyes.

Ghost quickly pulled Dana close and hugged her tightly. "You don't have to kill him, but you do need to separate yourself from him. You can even use me as an excuse if you need to."

For the next fifteen minutes Dana didn't speak, all she could do was cry her eyes out. Her entire life had just been flipped upside down.

*****

Stone stood enjoying his drink. He looked down at his watch and noticed that Dana had been gone for almost thirty minutes now. He was beginning to wonder if everything with her and her brother were all right. While

Stone waited for Dana to return he made his way over to the couch, where Randy sat and helped himself to a seat next to him.

"Come take a walk with me," Stone whispered leading Randy over to the kitchen area where they were alone. Once Stone was sure that the coast was clear, he reached up under Randy's shirt and snatched his wire off.

"Hey man, what are you doing?" Randy asked.

"Is Dana a part of your bank robber crew?" Stone asked.

Randy chuckled. "Apart of it?" he echoed. "Your little girlfriend and her brother are the masterminds of this whole operation," Randy said laughing. "Sleeping with the enemy, huh?"

"You better not had said shit to them about me!" Stone growled.

"They know nothing about you so relax," Randy said confidently.

Immediately, Stone's mind began to spin. There was no way his baby was a bank robber and murderer. Then he thought back on all the money that Dana had splurged since they met. He now knew where all the money came from. Just the thought of his girl being a part of something so negative made Stone sick to his stomach. He understood that some people weren't as fortunate as others were, so they had to do what they had to do, but when you begin to murder another human for money, that's where Stone had to draw the line. Stone had snatched Randy's wire from his chest so the other officers wouldn't find out about his involvement with a potential suspect. He had no clue who Dana really was, but something told him that he would soon find out. Stone turned his focus back on Randy. "You, Ghost, and Dana... Somebody is missing. Who's the fourth member?"

Randy nodded straight ahead. "See the guy with the blue hat on?"

"Yeah I see him."

"His name is Dougie and he's the final piece to the puzzle," Randy informed him.

Stone walked back over to the bar area and grabbed himself another drink. After all that he had discovered today, he had a lot to decide. In the back of his mind, he still couldn't believe that Dana could be affiliated with and a part of something so deadly and ruthless. He finally understood what it meant to not judge a book by the cover. Ten minutes later, he spotted Dana making her way over in his direction. Her face no longer looked friendly, but aggravated and frustrated.

"Hey baby everything okay?" Stone asked.

"No everything is not alright. I got something I need to take care of." She reached down in her purse, pulled out a hundred dollar bill, and handed it to Stone. "Catch a cab to your apartment and I'll meet you there in a few hours."

"Dana what's going on?" Stone asked with his voice full of concern.

"I'll explain everything tonight. Just please leave now," Dana told him.

Stone looked at Dana, turned, and then made his exit. He wasn't sure what was going on, but he definitely planned on getting to the bottom of it.

24

ONE LAST TIME

Once the party was over Ghost called an emergency meeting. His mind was all over the place now. Not only was he broke, but now his own sister was in love with the same detective that had tried to blow his head off. It just seemed like things were getting worse and worse. That's why Ghost planned on robbing this last bank and getting as far away from this lifestyle as he possibly could.

"What's this emergency meeting about?" Dougie was the first to speak. He didn't know what was going on, but from the look on Ghost's face, he could tell that whatever it was, it was serious.

"We're going to hit one last bank," Ghost announced. "And we're going to hit this bank in the next forty-eight hours.

"Why so soon?" Randy asked nosily.

"Because I think the cops may be on to us, so I say let's hit this last bank and strike while the iron is still hot."

"Which bank we hitting?" Randy asked. Everything was beginning to work out in his favor and in forty-eight hours, he would be a free man again.

"That fancy ass new bank downtown," Ghost replied. "I know we all have made a lot of money, so if anybody doesn't want to go through with this say so now and trust me, I fully understand," Ghost said letting his gaze land on Dana. "Everybody who's in, raise your hand."

Randy was the first to raise his hand followed by Dougie. All eyes in the room now focused on Dana. In Dana's heart, something didn't feel right about this job, but her brother needed her and there was no way she was going to let him down.

"I'm in," Dana said finally raising her hand.

25

MAKING A CHOICE

Stone sat in his apartment sipping on a glass of vodka, staring at the wall. He couldn't believe that the love of his life was a bank robber and murderer. His Dana wasn't who he thought she was. After the party, Randy informed Stone and his team about the when's and where's of the next bank job. Dana and her crew were now sitting ducks just waiting to be arrested and put in jail for the rest of their lives. Stone's thoughts were interrupted when he heard a soft knock at the door. "Who is it?"

"It's me," the voice on the other side of the door called out.

Stone opened the door and stepped to the side as he watched Dana enter his apartment with a sad look on her face. "You okay?"

"I could really use a drink baby," Dana said sadly.

"I got you baby," Stone said as he walked over to the kitchen and fixed Dana a drink. When he returned carrying the drink, he stopped mid-stride when he saw Dana standing with a gun pointed at his head. "So this is what it's come down to?"

"How long have you known about me?" Dana asked.

"I have known about your crew for weeks. I didn't find out about your involvement until tonight at the party," Stone told her. "Why Dana? Why?"

"Why didn't you tell me you were a cop from the beginning?"

"The same reason you didn't tell me you robbed banks for a living," Stone countered. "Listen to me Dana and I'm only going to tell you this because I love you. Leave town tonight and never come back. It's not too late for you to get away."

"You being a cop ruined our whole relationship," Dana said as tears ran down her eyes. "Why couldn't you just work at *Burger King* or something?"

"Your boy Randy is an informant," Stone came straight out and said it. He knew he shouldn't have told Dana this, but he loved her and he was trying to do everything in his power to persuade her not to rob that bank in a few days. "We know all about the bank robbery going down in a few days and we know everything that we need to know about all four of you," he said. "Please Dana, don't go through with this. Leave town and never come back." Stone inched his way towards her.

"Don't come any closer!" Dana shouted with the gun aimed at Stone's head. Stone ignored her threat and kept coming forward until he was close enough the grab the gun. Stone slowly grabbed the gun and gently removed it from Dana's hand.

"It's going to be okay," Stone said, pulling Dana in close and hugging her tight as she cried her eyes out. He understood her tough situation. Before Stone had decided to serve and protect, he had briefly been active in the streets, so he knew all about the struggle and being a product of one's environment. However, in order for one's actions to change, they had to change the way they thought first. Stone kissed Dana on the lips gently as he tossed her gun down on the couch and began to remove her pants. Stone laid Dana down on the coffee table, spread her legs apart, and began to slowly lick her pussy. Stone kissed, licked, and sucked on Dana's pussy as if it was the last time he would ever see her again. He sucked on her pussy as if he had just been released from prison after doing ten years, sucked on her pussy as if his life depended on it, sucked on her pussy as if he never wanted the moment to end. Dana's explosive orgasm took over her body as her legs began to tremble and lock around Stone's neck.

Stone then quickly turned Dana over on her stomach and entered her tight walls from behind. He started out with slow deep strokes, but when he got warmed up, Stone turned into an animal. He firmly gripped Dana's hips and tried to pulverize her insides. He watched as Dana's ass bounced and jiggled with each stroke he delivered until he couldn't take it any longer and exploded inside of Dana filling her with his fluids.

For the next thirty minutes, the two just laid there in silent listening to each other breathe.

"So I guess this is it, huh?" Dana said finally breaking the silence.

"It doesn't have to be baby," Stone said. "You can leave town now and we can keep in touch and you can enjoy your life and enjoy your money and I can even come and visit you once a month."

"What about my brother?" Dana asked. "He really needs the money," she said as tears began to fall from her eyes again.

"Money is not more important than one's freedom."

Dana got up and got dressed. "I have to do what I have to do and I don't expect you to understand."

"Fuck Ghost! You don't owe him shit!" Stone yelled. "He's going to get you killed Dana! Can't you see that?"

"Then so be it," Dana said as she grabbed her gun from off the couch and stuck it back in her purse. "Do yourself a favor and take a day off when we take this bank down because I won't hesitate to take you out," she warned.

"It's like that?" Stone asked with a hurt look on his face.

"This is the only way it can be baby." Dana leaned in and kissed Stone on the lips. "Take the day off, please! My team will shoot first and ask questions never! Please just take the day off, please!"

"I'm sorry, but I can't do that," Stone replied.

Dana looked him dead in the eyes. "I love you Stone," she said and then turned and made her exit.

"I love you too," Stone whispered as he watched Dana's *Benz* pull off. He hoped and prayed that in a couple of days, she changed her mind about taking down the bank with Ghost and her crew. Stone walked back over towards the couch and noticed a manila envelope sticking out of the cushion. "What the fuck?" he said to himself as he picked up the envelope and peeked inside at its contents. Inside he found $150,000 along with a letter. He quickly unfolded the letter and began to read it.

TIME IS MONEY

Dear Stone,

If you are reading this letter then that must mean that you know whom I really am now. lol Sorry for not being honest with you from the jump, but I really liked you and didn't want to scare you off. The funny thing is that when I met you, I told myself that I was out of the bank robbery business and was going to give this law abiding citizen thing a shot. lol Well I guess that wasn't what God had in his plans for me. This letter is to let you know that I love you more than anything in this whole world and if I disappointed you in anyway, I'm sorry. I enclosed $150k with this letter, because I want you to start living a little more and enjoy your life and you never know, maybe our paths may cross again in the future.

Your girl Dana.

I love you no matter what!

When Stone finished reading the letter, he felt immediately sorry for Dana. Her loyalty to her brother was going to get her killed. "I love you too baby," he whispered.

26

I SMELL A RAT

Dana pulled up in front of Ghost's house and beeped the horn. Something inside of her said that she should have killed Stone, but for some reason, she just couldn't do it. In spite of everything, she really loved him and didn't want to harm him. She wished that she could have somehow made things work with Stone, but knew that it was a dead end. Seconds later, Ghost entered the passenger seat with a relaxed look on his face. "What up?"

"We have a lot to talk about," Dana said pulling off. "First things first; Randy is a rat!"

Ghost laughed. "No way! We've been knowing him since forever."

"He's a rat!"

"You got proof?" Ghost asked.

"Stone told me."

"That's not proof," Ghost snapped. "That fucking cop is all in your head fucking up your judgment."

"Stone loves me and he wouldn't lie to me," Dana said defending Stone. "Plus why would he lie about Randy?"

"Divide and concur, that's the oldest trick in the book," Ghost's voice boomed. "He loves you," Ghost echoed with a disgusted look on his face. "You think he won't put a bullet in your head if the opportunity presents itself, because he damn sure tried to put a bullet in my head."

"He knows about the bank downtown," Dana said with an attitude. She had a feeling that Ghost wouldn't believe her when she told him the news.

"You told him about the job?" Ghost asked staring daggers into his little sister.

"Randy told him," she replied. "He's been acting funny lately anyway."

Ghost sat in the passenger seat quiet. Randy had been acting kind of funny lately, but not funny enough to where one would think that he was a rat. "You trust this cop that much?"

Dana nodded her head, "Yes."

"I can't afford to cancel this job," Ghost told her.

"Let's do it a day ahead of schedule," Dana suggested. "That way the cops won't have a beat on us."

"But for this job we are going to need four guys," Ghost said in deep thought.

"We can use Randy for the job and then kill him afterwards," Dana suggested.

"I just can't see Randy snitching," Ghost said sadly.

"Trust me," Dana said seriously. "He's a rat."

"Then he has to go," Ghost said. "And I'm sorry that your new boyfriend turned out to be a cop. I know you really liked him."

Dana flashed a hurt smile. "It is what it is."

"If Randy is working with the cops then we have to assume he told them about everything including the meet up house," Ghost said. "So that means we are going to have to switch it up."

"We can use my place as the meet up spot," Dana suggested.

"That'll work," Ghost said, sitting back in deep thought. He had to make sure he mapped everything out perfectly because all it took was one mistake for him and his sister to end up dead or either sitting in jail for the rest of their lives.

"What you over there thinking about?"

"I think we should take the bank first thing in the morning," Ghost said looking at Dana for a response. "That way we'll catch everyone off guard."

"That's going to be risky," Dana said looking directly at Ghost. "But, I think it can work."

Ghost smiled. "Let's do it!"

27

DON'T ASK ANY QUESTIONS

Dougie sat in the back of the stolen van listening as Ghost filled him in on all that was going on. He couldn't believe what he was hearing. When Ghost was finished, Dougie went on to tell him about the visit that Randy had made to his home about a week ago.

"I'm going to kill that snake myself," Ghost said. If it was one thing he hated, it was a snake. Over the years, Ghost had personally bailed Randy out of so many situations that it hurt him to hear that a person he called family had betrayed him.

Dougie placed a friendly hand on Ghost's shoulder. "It's going to be okay. You can't always expect other people to think or act like you do."

Dana pulled the van up in front of Randy's apartment and put the gear in park.

"I'll be back in a second," Ghost said hopping out the back of the van and headed in the building.

*****

Randy sat on the couch watching a porno when he heard someone banging on the door like the police. He looked over at the clock on the wall and it read 4:55 am. *"Who the fuck is knocking on my door this early in the morning?"* he said to himself as he got up and headed over to the front door. Randy looked through the peephole and saw Ghost standing on the other side.   "Hey Ghost what's up?" he said, stepping to the side so Ghost could enter. The first thing he noticed was that Ghost wasn't dressed in one of his expensive suits, but instead he wore all black and combat boots.

"Suit up," Ghost said looking Randy in the eyes. "I got another job for us. This is the one last final job."

"I thought we weren't supposed to hit the bank until two more days from now?"

"Change of plans," Ghost said quickly. "Go get dressed and I'll fill you in, in the car." He could tell by the uneasy look on Randy's face that something wasn't right. The plan was going according to plan. He could tell that his surprise visit had caught Randy off guard.

Fifteen minutes later Randy stepped back in the living room with a nervous look on his face. "Let's get this over with."

*****

Two blocks away a white van sat over in the cut. Two cops were assigned to keep an eye on Randy to make sure he didn't try to flee. The twenty-four hour surveillance paid off when one of the cops spotted Randy quickly coming out of the building and getting in the back of a van. The first thing the cop did was write down the license plate number. The second thing he did was dial Detective Anthony Stone's number. He had a feeling that something big was about to go down. "Follow that van," the cop that was in charge ordered.

28

NO TURNING BACK

When Stone got the call, he quickly hopped out of his bed. He had prayed the night before that Dana had taken his advice and decided to leave town and enjoy life, but when he got the call, he knew that she had done the exact opposite. Stone loved Dana, but he couldn't sit back and just let her continue to rob banks and kill people. Everyone had choices and Dana had chosen to not take Stone's advice and follow through with the heist. Stone weaved in and out of traffic like a mad man. He didn't want to hurt Dana, but if it came down to him and her, he planned on doing what he had to do. He pulled up behind the surveillance van; smoothly slipped out his car and hopped in the back of the van. "What did I miss?" he asked immediately.

"We followed their stolen van to that house five blocks down," the plain clothes cop explained. "I already got S.W.A.T. on standby and from the looks of it, it looks like something major is about to go down."

Stone pulled a bulletproof vest over his head and strapped it on as he processed what the cop had just told him. A part of him still hoped and wished that Dana would opt out of the deal before it was too late. *"Come on baby you are smarter than this,"* Stone said to himself.

29

TIME IS MONEY

"Today is business as usual," Ghost said, looking each one of his team members in the eyes. "We all know the rules. We get in and get what we can in three minutes; time is money!"

Under the table, in between Dana's legs, rested a book bag full of all the cash she had made on all the previous jobs. Once this job was over, she planned on leaving town immediately and never coming back. She had no clue where she was going. Her plan was to get on a plane and just go. All morning her mind had been on Stone and the last thing she wanted was for him to be disappointed in her, but at the end of the day her brother needed her and after all he had done for her over the years, there was no way she could tell him no.

"When this job is over we're all going to go our separate ways," Ghost coached. "We hot right now so I think it'll be best if we all get low for a while after this."

Members nodded their head in agreement.

Ghost looked over at Randy. "You got your strap on you?"

"Of course," Randy patted his waist.

"Good," Ghost smiled. "Change of plans, Randy you coming in with us this time," he said and then turned his attention to Dougie. "Dougie I'm going to need you to drive."

"I got you," Dougie replied. Ghost had already given him the heads up about Randy's foul ways and the thought of it all disgusted Dougie.

The foursome exited the house and hopped in the stolen van. The entire time, Ghost was secretly watching Randy. He kept a close eye on the snake in the grass. All morning Randy seemed nervous and jittery.

"You sure you want me to come inside the bank with ya'll?" Randy asked in a nervous tone.

"You been asking to get your hands dirty so now is your chance," Ghost said with a straight face. "Me and Dana will keep control of the place. All you have to do is fill these four duffle bags up with cash."

"I can handle that," Randy said in a shaky tone.

"You sure?" Ghost asked. "You look a little shaken up."

"I'm good, just a little tired. I been having trouble sleeping lately," Randy lied.

*****

Dougie pulled up across the street from the bank. "It's show time!" he announced.

"Everybody set your watch for three minutes," Ghost order as he tossed Randy, Dougie's, Ronald Reagan mask.

"Dougie, you better keep this van running!" Ghost ordered.

Dana slipped her Obama mask down over her face and grabbed her tech-9. She knew that once she put that mask on it was no turning back.

Ghost rolled his Bill Clinton mask down over his face, grabbed his M-16 rifle, and hopped out the back of the van leading his team into the bank.

*****

Stone watched from two blocks away as the heavily armed masked trio entered the bank. "Come on, we have to move now!" he ordered. Stone knew from watching the crew's previous bank robbery tapes that they liked to be in and out. His plan was to creep up on the bank robbers while they were still in the bank. He wanted his men to be in position, on the side of the building so that as soon as Ghost and his crew stepped foot out the bank, him and his team would be right there to apprehend them or worst case scenario his team would have to put them down.

Stone hopped out the back of the van with a machine gun in his hand. Behind him, ten heavily armed officers in riot gear followed his lead. Each member on Stone's team had been briefed on how dangerous the bank robbers were and they were all prepared to shoot at will.

The closer Stone made it to the side of the bank, the more his adrenalin began to pump. His palms were sweaty and clammy. His biggest fear had now become his reality. In a couple of minutes, the love of his life would be exiting the bank and it was sad to say, but Stone's mind was already made up. He would be shooting first and asking questions later.

30
THREE MINUTES

"Everybody on the fucking floor now!" Ghost yelled with his M-16 trained on the bank's security guard.

"You don't want to do this buddy. You're making a big mistake," the security guard warned.

Without warning Ghost blew the security guard's head off in front of everybody. He then quickly hopped up on the counter gaining control of the situation. "Let's move!"

Dana kept a close eye on all the tellers while Randy grabbed the manager and rushed her in the back room. She hoped and prayed that nobody pulled the silent alarm today because she was already in a bad mood and she wouldn't think twice about putting a bullet in someone's head.

"Bitch you better open this vault right motherfucking now!" Randy growled. The manager pulled the keys from her pocket, but couldn't get her hand to stop shaking. "Bitch!" Randy barked as he back slapped the manager down to the floor, scooped the keys up off the floor, and let himself into the vault. Once inside the vault, Randy began to fill up all four duffle bags.

*****

Dougie sat behind the wheel of the stolen van with a nervous look on his face. He wasn't used to sitting outside. He was used to being on the inside around all of the action. Every car that drove by, Dougie swore that they were the police. Ever since he found out that Randy was working with the cops, he just knew that in any second, the place was going to be surrounded by cops. Just when Randy's nerves began to settle down he spotted movement from the corner of his eye. He looked over and saw cops dressed in riot gear creeping up on the side of the bank. "Shit!" Dougie cursed as he grabbed the A.K. 47 that rested on the floor and quickly hopped out the van and opened fire on the police.

BRAT, TAT, TAT, TAT, TAT, TAT, TAT!

*****

Once Stone and his team got into position, a burst of gunfire sounded off loudly. Stone watched as two members from his team were gunned down in cold blood. He quickly took cover behind a parked car as bullets pinged loudly off the car. His team quickly returned fire turning the one sided gun battle into a shootout.

Dougie sprung from behind the van opening fire on the cops. He could have easily driven away and escaped on his own, but there was no way he was going to leave his team and let them get ambushed by the cops. That just wasn't how he was brought up. He quickly ducked down behind the van as the cops returned fire.

Dougie popped up from behind the van again and opened fire, but this time a bullet ripped through his shoulder and then his thigh causing him to drop down to the ground behind the van. He looked down and saw a big hole in his leg and blood everywhere. He tried to reach over and grab his gun off the ground, but when he looked up, he saw two cops standing over him. Instead of reading him his rights, they put a bullet in his head instead.

31

TIME TO GO

Ghost looked down at his watch and so far only a minute and a half had passed. He walked back and forth keeping a close eye on all of the bank employees. Today he didn't want any innocent people to lose their lives. Ghost was about to yell something to Dana when he heard what sounded like a million different guns being fired outside. He hopped off the counter, looked out the front door, and saw Dougie shooting it out with several police officers. The first thing that popped into Ghost's mind was Randy. Ghost had made sure he kept a close eye on all the employees so he knew there was no way that the cops would be there that fast without the silent alarm being pulled. More gunshots ringing out snapped Ghost out of his thoughts. Outside sounded like the Fourth of July. Right on queue Randy came running out of the back carrying four duffle bags, two in each hand.

"What's going on?" Randy asked as if he had no clue on what was going down. "Who shooting?"

Ghost quickly turned his M-16 on Randy. "What kind of man would set his own family up?"

"Ghost you bugging! You know I would never do no shit like that," Randy lied with a straight face.

Ghost shook his head sadly, as he pulled down on the trigger. It hurt him to watch the bullets rip through Randy's body like a wet paper bag.

"Come on we have to go!" Dana said as she quickly picked up two duffle bags and placed them over her shoulder. She knew that when Ghost killed Randy it would be like losing a brother, but at the end of the day,

Randy had to go. Ratting out your family was unacceptable!

Ghost grabbed the two remaining duffle bags as him and Dana headed for the exit. "I'll cover you," Ghost said as he exited the bank and opened fire on the police while Dana ran and hid behind a parked car.

The M-16 rattled in Ghost's hand as shell case after shell case popped out the side of the rifle. He watched as his M-16 bullets had cops dropping like flies. When he ran out of bullets, Dana popped up from behind the parked car and opened fire on the cops giving Ghost time to join her behind the parked car.

Ghost hid behind the car as he slammed a fresh clip in the base of his gun. "Come we gotta go!" He sprung from behind the car and squeezed down on the trigger as him and Dana quickly back peddled over towards the getaway van.

Dana tossed her two duffle bags in the back and hopped behind the wheel of the van. As she climbed in the van, she stepped over Dougie's dead body. She hated to have to leave his body lying in the street like that, but she didn't have time to grab him. "Come on Ghost!"

Ghost opened the side door to the van, tossed his duffle bags in the back, and then went back and scooped up Dougie's body and laid him in the back of the van as bullets pinged loudly off the body of the van. Once Ghost was in the van, Dana stomped down on the gas pedal flying away from the crime scene.

"You almost got us killed!" Dana yelled.

"I couldn't just leave Dougie's body in the middle of the street like that!" Ghost replied.

"What's the plan now?" Dana asked as she drove recklessly through the streets. "Hold on! Do you hear that?"

"Hear what?"

"Shhh, listen," Dana said. The sound of a helicopter hovering over them could be heard loud and clear. "A helicopter."

"Shit!" Ghost cursed as he stuck his head out the window and looked up into the air. There it was, a helicopter following them and reporting their every move. Without thinking twice, Ghost grabbed his M-16, hung half his body out the window, and opened fire on the helicopter. Immediately the helicopter flew out of range.

"We got company!" Dana yelled out. Behind the van, three cop cars trailed and a black *Charger* brought up the rear. Immediately Dana recognized the *Charger*. It was the same color, make, and model of Stone's *Charger*. "Get them off our ass!"

Ghost repositioned himself halfway out the window and opened fire on the squad cars that trailed. The M-16 bullets tore through the squad cars like a hot knife through butter.

"Shoot out their tires!" Dana yelled.

Ghost aimed his M-16 down at the tires of the cop cars and squeezed down on the trigger, swaying his arms back and forth.

Dana watched through the rearview mirror as one of the squad cars lost control and crashed into another squad car causing a huge accident in the middle of the intersection.

"Take us to the Greyhound station," Ghost instructed.

"What?"

"Do what I say!"

"There's no way we're going to be able to escape on no damn Greyhound bus!" Dana snapped.

"Dana this is New York!" Ghost told her. "There's going to be thousands of people at the Greyhound station, not to mention the subway is down there along with at least twenty different exits. We'll have a good chance at blending in with the crowd and getting away," he explained.

Dana was about to respond when movement in the rearview mirror caught her eye. "Shit we got more company!" she announced as the black *Charger* began to pick up speed and close the distance between the two.

32

NO WAY OUT

Stone weaved around the huge accident at the intersection and continued his pursuit. The way Ghost and Dana had shot and killed cops as if it was nothing, truly disturbed him. He never would have thought that Dana truly was this type of person that. It hurt Stone's heart to know that a woman he loved would soon be murdered or spending the rest of her life in jail. There was nothing he could do to help Dana. She had officially reached the point of no return. As Stone tailed the van, he noticed a figure with a Bill Clinton mask stick his arm out the window and open fire on him.

Stone ducked down right on time as bullets tore through and shattered his windshield. Once the gunfire ended, Stone quickly removed his 9mm from its holster, stuck his arm out the window, and fired several shots into the body of the van. He had told himself that he wouldn't use his firearm unless he was left with no choice.

Stone looked down at his speedometer that read 98 mph. He followed the van until it came to a complete stop downtown at 42nd street. He watched as two figures hopped out the van wearing mask and carrying duffle bags. The duo fired a few shots into his windshield before disappearing in the port authority entrance of the station.

Stone grabbed his walkie-talkie, called in for back up, reloaded his gun, and headed inside the port authority entrance after the brother and sister duo.

33
BY ANY MEANS
NECESSARY

Once inside the station, Ghost and Dana removed their masks and tossed them in the garbage as they quickly blended in with the New York crowd.

"We have to split up," Ghost said as he grabbed Dana and hugged her tightly. "I love you!"

"How will we keep in contact if we split up?" Dana asked in a panic.

"Don't worry about that. I'll find you," Ghost said, flashing his signature smile. "Love you and if you go down don't go down without a fight," he said as he hugged her again. Then the two quickly turned and walked in opposite directions as if they didn't know one another.

Dana power walked through the station until she reached the escalator. She wondered if this were the last time, that she would see her brother ever again. This entire heist didn't play out the way it had played out in her mind. Everything that could have gone wrong did. Dana made her way over to the counter and ordered a one way ticket to Atlanta.

"Ma'am there's a bus leaving for Atlanta in thirty minutes," the man behind the counter told her. "You can catch that bus or the next one leaves two hours from now."

"I'll take the one that leaves in thirty minutes," Dana said quickly as she kept glancing over her shoulder. When she got her ticket, she swiftly walked over to one of the small shops in the station and purchased a floppy hat. She used the hat as a form of disguise as she headed to the gate number that was printed out on her ticket. When Dana reached the gate, her eyes lit up when she saw that they were already boarding. *"Thank you Jesus!"* she said to herself as she stood on the end of the line and boarded the bus.

34

I AIN'T GOING OUT
LIKE NO SUCKER

G host walked swiftly through the station. He was beginning to feel like robbing this last bank was a bad idea. He didn't know how, but he was determined to make it out of this situation alive and with his freedom. With each step that Ghost took, it felt like every eye in the terminal was watching him. Ghost walked into one of the gift shops and purchased a pair of sunglasses. He knew that the cops more than likely knew what he looked like, so he needed some form of disguise. As Ghost walked through the station, one of the straps on his duffle bag broke. "Shit!" he cursed. Ghost quickly headed to a nearby rest room. He looked under the stalls and saw a pair of feet in the last stall. Ghost quickly walked over to the last stall and kicked the door open.

Boom!

He roughly snatched the man up off the toilet, slapped the shit out of him, and then forced him out of the restroom.

Ghost's plan was to open both duffle bags and see if there were any small bills in either of the bags. He would then place all the big bills in the good duffle bag and leave the rest in the bathroom for a lucky someone to find it. Ghost opened the first duffle bag and began to go through the bills when a dye pack exploded in his face.

"What the fuck?" Ghost said with a confused look on his face. He looked up in the mirror and saw that his face, shirt, and hands had been covered in red dye. He looked down and saw that the money was also covered in red dye. "Noooooo!" Ghost yelled as he tossed the bag across the bathroom sending money flying all over the place. Another man entered the restroom, but stopped mid-stride when he saw what was going on in the bathroom. He quickly spun around and walked right back out.

Ghost grabbed the other duffle bag and began to fish through the bills when another dye pack exploded. He continued to look through the bag to see if any bills hadn't been soiled, but he had no such luck. "Fuck!" he cursed loudly. Ghost turned the water on and washed his face the best he could, but his face was still covered in dye. He exited the restroom and hurried down towards the subway. He couldn't believe that all the hard work he had went through had all been for nothing. He now had no family and no money. Everything he had worked so hard for was all for nothing.

35

I SEE YOU

S tone walked through the terminal with his gun out. He held it behind his thigh as not to draw attention to it. With so many people roaming around the station, it made it hard for Stone to pin point who he was looking for. He scanned through the sea of faces and came up empty. As he walked through the station, a man bumped into him. "Hey, watch where you are going!"

"I'm sorry mister but can I use your phone for a second. I need to call the police. There's a man in the bathroom right now with bags full of money and blood everywhere," the man said, confusing the red dye for blood.

"What bathroom?" Stone asked.

"That one right there," the man pointed.

Stone quickly hurried in the direction of the bathroom. As he got close to the bathroom, Stone spotted Ghost quickly heading down the stairs to the subway. Stone slowly jogged after Ghost. There was no way he was going to allow him to escape as he did the last time. The last thing Stone wanted to do was to have a shootout in a crowded subway station, but if it came down to it then so be it. Stone jogged until he got around fifteen feet away from Ghost before he yelled, "Ghost!"

Immediately Ghost spun around. His face crumbled up as soon as he saw Stone's face.

"Down on the floor now!" Stone ordered as he inched in closer. Innocent bystanders immediately began to scream hysterically when they saw Stone's gun. "Don't make me shoot you because I will!" Stone warned. "Down on the floor, now!"

Ghost smiled. "You know my sister really loves you. I would have killed you myself, but the only reason I didn't was because of her," he told the detective.

"Ghost please don't make me do it," Stone begged. "Get down on the floor! NOW!"

"Fuck you!" Ghost said as he went for the P89 in his waistband. Before he could even reach the handle, four shots exploded in his chest in a rapid succession dropping him instantly.

Stone inched his way over to Ghost's body and checked his pulse. "Damn!" he said when he didn't feel a pulse. He felt bad about killing Dana's brother, but he had no other choice then to do what he had to do.

36
I ALMOST GOT AWAY WITH IT

D ana sat on the bus staring blankly out the window. All she wanted was for the bus to hurry up and pull out of the station. It seemed as if the bus driver was doing everything, but getting in the driver's seat and pulling off. As Dana sat on the bus, she wondered how Ghost was holding up right now. Had he gotten away? Had the cops murdered him? Would she ever speak to or see him again? Those were all the questions that ran through Dana's mind. Finally, the bus driver boarded the bus and got behind the wheel. He drove about ten to fifteen feet away before he stopped. Dana then heard his voice over the loud speaker.

"Sorry passengers, but I've been ordered to not leave the terminal. It seems as if the cops are demanding that they check all buses before they depart. I'm sorry for the delay and the inconvenience."

Dana's heart immediately leaped into her throat after hearing that message from the driver. She just knew that it was over for her. Tears rolled down her face as she pulled her 9mm from her waist and sat it on her lap with her shirt covering it. If she was going out, she definitely wasn't going to go quietly.

*****

Stone made his way back upstairs and saw Captain Fisher standing there with an angry look on his face.

"Good work back there Stone," Fisher began. "But there's still one missing and I think she's on one of these buses. No bus is to leave until it has been thoroughly searched!"

"Copy," Stone replied as he walked out to the loading dock. He immediately saw armed officers searching all of the buses. "Hey which one of these buses hasn't been searched yet?" he asked a uniform officer.

"Those three right there haven't been searched yet sir," the officer told him.

"I'll take care of it," Stone said. He reached the first bus and reloaded his gun before he boarded it.

Stone slowly walked down the aisle on the bus looking from face to face. The whole time he walked the aisle, he prayed that he didn't see Dana. After searching the entire bus, Stone walked back to the front of the bus. "You're clear to go," he told the driver as he hopped off that bus and hopped straight onto the next bus. Stone slowly walked up the aisle looking at each and every passengers face carefully. Once he was sure that Dana wasn't on this bus either, he walked back to the front of the bus and told the driver, "You're clear to go." Then he exited the bus. Stone quickly headed over to the last bus and boarded it. He slowly made his way down the aisle looking from face to face, making sure that he kept his 9mm down by his side. His face was covered in sweat. He didn't realize how hot it was in the bus terminal until now. Stone slowly eased his way down the aisle and stopped when he spotted Dana sitting in a window seat with a big floppy hat on her head. He looked and saw tears running down her eyes. Her eyes told Stone that she was sorry, told him that she still loved him, told him that she was human, and had made a mistake. Stone continued down the aisle as if he didn't see Dana sitting there. He then made his way back to the front of the bus and told the driver, "You're clear to go." Stone hopped off the bus and watched as it slowly pulled off. Stone made eye contact with Dana as the bus was pulling off and he saw Dana mouth the words, "I love you."

"I love you too baby," Stone mouthed back as he watched the bus pull out of the station. It was at that moment that he knew that he would never see or hear from Dana again. Stone knew the real Dana, the loving and caring Dana. Inside he felt like he had done the right thing because he believed in second chances and he knew that he had saved Dana's life the same way she had saved his by not letting Ghost kill him.

"What a day," Stone said to himself as he headed for his car to go home and get some much needed rest.

37

THREE WEEKS LATER

After a long day of work, Stone stepped out of his car, checked the mail, and headed upstairs to his apartment. The first thing he did when he got upstairs was pour himself a strong, stiff drink. He then looked through his mail that he knew would be nothing but bills. Stone paused when he came across a posted letter that was addressed to him with no return address. He quickly opened the letter and began to read.

Hey Stone, this letter is just to say thank you. I really appreciate what you did for me. You taught me that there is such a thing as real love. I know that we more than likely will never see one another again so this letter is just to let you know that I appreciate you and because of you, I have officially turned my life around and used my second chance at life to do some good for once. I will always love you no matter what and you will always hold a special place in my heart.

Yours truly,

Dana

I love you!

Stone read the letter and all he could do was smile. He was happy that Dana had changed her life around for the better. It was too bad that it took her losing her entire family to finally come to this conclusion. Stone looked

down at the letter and said, *"I love you too baby."*

THE END!

New Release

48 Hours to Die: An Anthony Stone Novel

by Silk White

Books by Good2Go Authors on Our Bookshelf

Good2Go Films Presents

To order books, please fill out the order form below:
To order films please go to www.good2gofilms.com

Name: _____

Address: _____

City: _____ State: _____ Zip Code: _____

Phone: _____

Email: _____

Method of Payment: ☐ Check   ☐ VISA   ☐ MASTERCARD

Credit Card#: _____

Name as it appears on card: _____

Signature: _____

Item Name	Price	Qty	Amount
48 Hours to Die – Silk White	14.99		
He Loves Me, He Loves You Not - Mychea	$14.99		
He Loves Me, He Loves You Not 2 - Mychea	$14.99		
He Loves Me, He Loves You Not 3 - Mychea	$14.99		
Married To Da Streets – Silk White	$14.99		
My Boyfriend's Wife - Mychea	$14.99		
Never Be The Same – Silk White	$14.99		
Stranded – Silk White	$14.99		
Slumped – Jason Brent	$14.99		
Tears of a Hustler - Silk White	$14.99		
Tears of a Hustler 2 - Silk White	$14.99		
Tears of a Hustler 3 - Silk White	$14.99		
Tears of a Hustler 4- Silk White	$14.99		
Tears of a Hustler 5 – Silk White	$14.99		
Tears of a Hustler 6 – Silk White	$14.99		
The Panty Ripper - Reality Way	$14.99		
The Teflon Queen – Silk White	$14.99		
The Teflon Queen 2 – Silk White	$14.99		
The Teflon Queen – 3 – Silk White	$14.99		
The Teflon Queen 4 – Silk White	$14.99		
Time Is Money - Silk White	$14.99		
Young Goonz – Reality Way	$14.99		
Subtotal:			
Tax:			
Shipping (Free) U.S. Media Mail:			
Total:			

Make Checks Payable To: Good2Go Publishing - 7311 W Glass Lane, Laveen, AZ 85339

CPSIA information can be obtained at www.ICGtesting.com
Printed in the USA
LVOW10s2126090115

422241LV00012B/101/P

9 780692 275962